Friends Forever

Friends Forever

By Marilyn Martin

Four Seasons Publishers
Titusville, FL

Friends Forever

For information contact: Four Seasons Publishers
P.O.Box 51, Titusville, FL 32781

PRINTING HISTORY
First Printing 2000

ISBN 1-891929-58-5

PRINTED IN THE UNITED STATES OF AMERICA
1 2 3 4 5 6 7 8 9 10

Dedications and Acknowledgements

This book is dedicated to the memory of my Danish grandfather, Soren Paulson Aagaard.
Thank you dear "Gramp" for instilling in me a love of animals and nature. You were the best! Also to the memory of my parents, Stanley A. Aagaard, Sr. and Ethel E. Smith Aagaard.
All three remain forever in my heart and ever in my soul.

My deepest gratitude goes to my husband, Evan, for his love and unwavering support. Dearest Ev, you alone have made this book possible. I love you more than ever.

Thank you also to our children, David Evan Martin, and Laura Elizabeth Martin, and our daughter-in-law, Susan Lynn Garrick Martin. Your interest in this project has kept me going. Love to you for all of your help and kind thoughts.

For the best editor in the world, Julia Lee Dulfer. I have learned to love the art of writing more than ever! And now I feel the same way about the craft of editing.
All because of you, J.L. Thanks for your encouragement!

To my brother, Stan Aagaard: My thanks and love for your thoughts and interest, dear bro!

To Russ Taylor for the fine illustrations. Great job, Russ! I really enjoyed working with you.

Thank you to all who helped me with my research at Horses for the Handicapped in Melbourne, Florida; especially director Pamela Rogan. Dear Pam, you are just wonderful at what you do. My thanks! Also my gratitude to Faye Holden and all of the gentle people and children that look forward to their weekly rides on their favorite horse.

Thanks to my friend, Duane Yotti, for her idea about Cody's bucket of minnows!

IN MEMORIAM: The chapter titled, Step Two, is dedicated to Patricia Daly, "the Tree Lady."

And to the rest of the world!--This has been some ride! I would not have missed it for anything!

Marilyn

Book I

Alexandra

Alexandra

Up early and perched on the back porch railing, Alexandra listened to the morning noises. Freedom, with the whole summer vacation ahead of her! All she needed was an interesting project to keep her busy. Maybe some time on her old swing would help her think.

Pumping hard, she sailed into the air. Her silky, red-blonde hair glistened in the brilliant Colorado sun. From on high, she spotted something moving at the edge of the creek down the hill. Curious, she dragged her feet to slow down and jumped off. She was now able to hear a small animal crying in distress. Another pitiful howl made her want to cry too. Stepping quickly through the yard, she headed toward the source of trouble.

She sped down the well-worn path through the trees. Her flying legs sent clouds of little bugs skittering from the grassy verge as she ran. Pushing through the red-willow bushes she climbed onto a large, flat-topped rock to scan the creek. Right below her a small golden puppy struggled, mired to its chest in the muddy

mess left by last weekend's flood.

"Oh, you poor thing!" The pup raised its head toward the welcome voice, sensing rescue had arrived.

Gently, so as to not frighten it, Alex knelt, extended her hand and offered soothing encouragement. The puppy whimpered and wriggled, desperately trying to free its legs.

"Hold still," Alex pleaded. "I'll be right back with help." She jumped off the rock and ran home helter-skelter. The pup yowled and tried even harder to free itself from the gluey mud.

Alexandra got her rubber boots and grabbed her grandfather's fishnet from their dusty shed.

"Mother! Gramp!" she called as she came out. "Come down to the creek and help me!"

Busy vacuuming, her mother didn't hear her. Gramp, shaving in the upstairs bathroom, didn't either. The only one who did was Chester, the family dachshund. He'd been snoozing on his rug in the kitchen. Chet woke with a start at the sound of Alexandra's voice. The chocolate-brown doxie's short, strong front legs pushed hard on the screen door. It burst open, and out he zipped in determined pursuit of Alex.

As she shot down the path, her baseball cap flew off. Her shiny black boots galumphed along, and her heart was pounding as fast as her feet. The frightened puppy was now up to its chin in the sticky mud.

Chester, skinny little tail whirring, chased along with his nose radaring her scent. Getting close, Alex heard the creek singing a soft song as it flowed over the smooth stones. She heard nothing else. Peering around the rock, she spotted the silent little dog.

"Oh, my goodness! Wake up, puppy." Alex called, but it did not respond.

Sick with worry, she dropped the fishnet and hung on to an overhanging branch. She lowered herself off the rock and down into the muck, one foot at a time. Squish! Thinking fast, Alex pulled on a boot top. A loud slur-r-r-p and the boot popped free. She stepped and tugged, getting closer inch by inch. Alex leaned down to scoop the mud away from the little dog.

"How did you ever get into this mess?" she asked.

Chester huffed and puffed his elongated body up onto the rock to see what was going on. He turned and scurried back home to alert the family with his shrill barking.

"You're going to make it. Just please wake up," she crooned to the pup as she worked. It stirred and lifted its tired head. Paw by paw, Alex freed the dog from its boggy trap. She picked it up and hugged it tight, mud and all, as it softly licked her cheek.

"Sweet baby, I bet you're happy to be out of that nasty goo," she said.

Alex tried to take a step toward the bank, but she was stuck fast! And she couldn't pull on the boots while holding the pup.

Okay, now what do I do? Alex grinned as she thought of a solution. Wiggling her toes, she raised one leg. Out of the boot came her foot in its lacy white sock.

Alex sank it into the mud. Next came the other foot. With a few more squishy steps she reached the rock.

"Phew! We made it!" Out of breath, she sat and rocked the shivering bundle in her arms.

Her mother and Gramp came tearing along the path with Chester chuffing in their wake carrying Alexandra's cap clenched in his teeth.

"Here we are!" shouted Alex.

"We? Who's we?" Anne Tanner called out. They found her with the tiny creature clasped in her arms.

"Oh, Alexandra, what is that? What have you been up to?"

Alex patiently answered all their questions and added one of her own: "May I keep the puppy? Please?"

Anne was so relieved to find her safe that she didn't even scold. On the way home Gramp checked for a collar or identification tag but found none.

"We'll try to find out who owns it," he said. "I suspect we're too far out in the country for the dog to be lost."

"What do you mean, Gramp?" asked Alex.

"Sometimes people don't want their pets, so they abandon them far away from home," he explained.

"They don't want them? I can't believe anyone would do that! Well, I want it! Mom, if I can keep the puppy, I promise to feed and care for it and work on training it. That could be my summertime project. I bet it would be the best one ever. What do you say?" she asked. "Oh, I just thought of something. What is puppy, a boy or a girl?"

"She's a beautiful female. With this color she must have a lot of golden retriever in her," Gramp Tanner said. "When she's cleaned up, she'll be a blonde beauty just like you! I'm real proud of you for rescuing her, honey."

"I like your idea, Alex," said her mother. "It's a good one. I think the pup will keep you busy."

"Do you think Chester will mind having another dog around?" Alex asked.

Hearing his name, Chester looked up. He'd been busy sniffing Alexandra's dirty socks. When Alex showed him the puppy, he gave a rousing, "Yip! Yip! Yip!" and a happy tail spin! Gramp laughed. "There's your answer."

"I think they'll be great friends," said Alex, "and Goldilocks will always have a loving family to care for her."

Sleigh Ride

Snow dusted from pine boughs by the flick and swish of the horses' tails danced on the crisp winter air to the rhythm of freshly polished silver bells. Twisting about, Alexandra lifted her face to catch the stinging icy stars.

It was a beautiful day for a family tradition, a Christmas afternoon sleigh ride along the frozen creek and over the meadows and hills behind the ranch.

Steven Tanner perched up front on the high seat of the old wagon onto which he and Gramp had fastened runners. He was bundled in a sheepskin jacket and layers of warm blankets. A red Santa cap covered his ears, its furry tassel dangling at a jaunty angle as he drove. He skillfully guided the two Belgian draft horses through the holiday's gift of new-fallen snow. In their thick winter coats, Susie and Sally were a pair of caramel-colored beauties.

Alex sat in back, toasty warm in her new quilted jumpsuit. Along with Mom, Gramp, and Chester, she was tucked into a cocoon of heavy, wool covers. The little dog's nose barely poked

out for air.

Chet dearly loved to hitch a ride on anything that moved faster than he could run. With his stubby legs, deep snow posed a serious hazard during his daily exercise sessions.

"Chester's content," Gramp said. "He knows the horses can't bother him back here".

"Don't worry, he'll pop up when he smells the wild animals," Mom replied. "Young Goldilocks would love this. We'll have to take her on our next outing."

"Come on, let's sing!" Alex's dad called.

The sound of "Jingle Bells" rang out across the meadow's white mantle. The sleigh moved faster, with the horses' bobbing heads keeping time to the rousing tune.

"Look!" Alex said and nudged Gramp. In the distance a small herd of mule deer pawed at the drifts, foraging for tufts of dried grass. They lifted their heads and blinked soft brown eyes at the carolers' sleigh.

Dad tugged on the reins, drawing the horses to a halt. Gramp and Alex hopped off and pulled a bale of hay from the tailgate. Gramp broke it open with his knife, and they spread the fodder for the hungry deer to munch.

"I'll get them a few scoops of dried alfalfa meal for dessert," she said, wrinkling her nose at the thought. "I'm glad my cereal doesn't smell like this!" She trampled down an area and sprinkled around the compressed pellets.

"I bet they'll hightail it to the feast as soon as we leave," Alex said, stopping for a moment to gaze across the meadow. "I love helping animals; it's such a great feeling."

"Me, too," Gramp told her. "My father and I did it every winter. In autumn we'd gather and store our provisions in a cave in the hillside. He'd dug it out and mounted a door long before I was born. Covered with layers of straw, the food would keep all year. Any extras we had during the hardest winter times, we'd share with the animals," he said.

"Come on. We'll probably find more—maybe some elk."

Giving her arm a quick squeeze he boosted her into the sleigh.

"Merry Christmas!" Mom called to the waiting deer.

They continued on into the low-lying hills. Their destination was a secret known only to Steven. Susie and Sally, who knew the route by heart, carefully made their way along the creek that here and there showed patches of rushing indigo water.

"Where are we going?" Alex leaned forward to watch her father work with the team across dangerous patches of ice.

"You'll soon find out," her dad answered, allowing the reins to run loosely in his hands, again letting the horses pick their own way across the flatlands. The others shared a look that said they had guessed his secret.

"How are you feeling, Mom? Alex sat back and smoothed the covers over her mother's lap. "Are you all right?" She had good reason to ask. Late in the spring her mother was going to have a baby, and Alex felt very protective.

"I'm fine, honey."

The doxie awakened and edged his paws up Alexandra's chest, demanding attention. "Next year, Chettie, our baby will come with us."

"Woof!" he seemed to answer and pushed a scratchy, sleep-dried nose at her chin. She laughed and hugged him tight.

Spotting elk and big horn sheep, Dad stopped the sleigh several times. Alex and Gramp spread hay and distributed bushels of stored apples, corn, and concentrated food pellets. Chester jumped down with an apple clamped in his jaws. Careful to stay in Alex's tracks, he gave a menacing growl at the huge horses as they skirted the leggy team that seemed to grow larger each time he ventured near them.

"I think Chester in the snow makes a perfect shot for our album," Mom said, taking pictures with her new camera.

"I'm glad he's not a white dog—we'd never find the little bugger!" Alex shouted.

Time out for a picnic was called, and they feasted on homemade apple pie with icing and mugs of hot cocoa. Though Chester snacked heartily on the leftovers, his favorite treat was that shiny red apple. Tummy bulging, he once again snuggled down in his warm nest.

"Whoa there!" The team's hooves crunched to a halt as Alex popped up and stood gazing at the dazzling scene.

"I know this place! It's the beaver pond. We came here late last summer when they were busy storing food for winter. It's frozen solid! Where are they now?"

Dad set the brake pole and hooked the reins around it before jumping down to stretch his cramped legs.

"Looks different, huh, Al?" he said.

"It sure does. I pictured rocks and sticks showing through the snow, but look at the lodge—it's just a big white mound! Can we get near it?"

"Well, the ice is strong enough, so we can go and have a look," said Gramp, helping them down.

Chester, nose to the ground and tail waving like a frantic pinwheel, quickly sniffed out a host of delicious smells. Alex soon discovered what he was so excited about.

"Look at all those tracks. I hope the beavers are safe," she said.

"I see them—lynx, wolverine, cougar, and maybe even fox," Gramp said. Steven nodded in agreement and knelt down to take a closer look.

"Like the deer and elk herds, they're searching for food. Some of them won't make it through the winter."

"Let's see if the lodge has been broken into," Gramp said.

Alex went closer to search for signs of damage. She ran her mittened hand over the packed, paw-printed snow.

"I can't find any holes. They've dug and scratched at it, but it still feels tight," she announced.

"I'm curious," her mother said. "See if you hear anything in there." So Alex pushed her earmuff aside and bent close to the domed top of the beavers' home. As everyone waited expectantly, a sleek black raven arrived. Head and shiny ebony beak pointed downward, ever searching, it gave a raucous "caw-caw," indignant at the sight of human intruders.

"We heard that!" laughed Mom.

All except Alex were startled by the racket. They turned back to see a smile slide across her face.

"I hear little chattering noises," Alex murmured. Her right ear seemed frozen to the spot.

"Ah, they're awake and having a Christmas party, too," Mom said.

"Maybe the parents dove down to their storage area for some tasty willow roots or aspen twigs," said Dad.

"It's frozen. How could they do that?" asked Alexandra.

"They keep entrance and exit holes in the den floor open all winter to get to their food supply below. In the fall they stock up by anchoring branches in the mud or weighting them down with rocks. That way they and their babies don't starve."

"They have little ones in there now?" Alex asked.

"They probably do, honey. The kits stay with the family for two years. A female beaver gets pregnant in late winter and carries her next babies for about three months. They're born in April or May, and the older ones help take care of them. She'll have two or three babies, maybe even four," Dad said. "It'll be a full house!"

Alex gave her mother a warm hug. "You're going to have your baby in May, too, just like a beaver!" she said, her eyes sparkling with amusement.

"We'll have to come back here then, Alex, to check for the yearlings and try to get a glimpse of the brand new kits learning to swim," her grandfather said.

"I'd really like that, Gramp," said Alexandra, already dreaming of the spring to come.

Spring Promise

"Hooray! Today's the day you promised we'd ride to the beaver pond," Alexandra called to her grandfather between hops and skips. Hands planted firmly on her hips, she stomped her scuffed white boots together on the packed earthen floor of the horse barn and grinned up at him.

"Hey, Gramp, this is it! We're outta here!"

Alex jammed a scarf and gloves into an empty pocket and paused. True to form, her grandfather tilted his slate-colored head, and set his hearty laugh bouncing off the rough-sawn roof beams. She was wrapped in a cocoon of happiness.

"Yes, and a good morning to you, dear Alexandra. Something on your mind this early in the day?" he teased, brushing glints of moisture from the corners of his eyes.

"You know! Beavers are taking a snappy trip through my brain right now."

She dragged in deep breaths to absorb the familiar scent of horses, polished leather, and fresh hay piled in the new pinewood stalls.

"This place has a wonderful warmth, doesn't it?" Gramp said, ruffling Alex's hair. "It's a great feeling on a chilly morning before dawn." Colorado weather liked to play seasonal ping-pong in the Rockies. It didn't dampen her enthusiasm one bit.

"I can't believe we're getting close to the end of May," Alex chattered. "There are piles of delicious looking whipped-cream snow still hanging on the peaks. Maybe we'll get to ride through some leftovers on the trail. Wouldn't that be super?" She whistled a cheery tune as she hustled to the tack room to grab a saddle and bridle.

"I want to see the year-old kits again and find out if there are any new babies. I've crossed all of my fingers and toes." She stood on a step stool to lay the black-and-red Indian saddle pad on Jessie, her palomino.

"It's supposed to stay nice, so we ought to have a great time," Gramp said. His sharp eyes caught the way she eased the bit into Jess's mouth. He propped his leg on a barrel, leaned elbow to knee, and waited for James, his favorite thoroughbred, to exhale before tightening the cinches.

"Come on, big guy, relax so we can get the saddle tight." He continued to whisper into the horse's fuzz-trimmed ears. They pricked and swiveled back to catch the soft sound of his words. James shuffled about and thought it over. He flipped his long tail and finally, bored with it all, released a lengthy gust from his nose.

"I heard that, he's ready now!" Alex called from the neighboring stall.

"Thank goodness, you old nag," Gramp said. James lipped his suede vest, now ready to settle the whole matter. With a rewarding pat on the horse's strong, glossy neck, Gramp unhooked his Stetson from its peg, tugged the brim down and bent to recheck his equipment.

Alex jumped from the stool and gave it a kick to get it away from Jessie. Other resident horses lifted their heads from troughs of breakfast grain and pawed at the straw-covered floor, anxious to be noticed too.

"I'm all set. I have my bed roll and the rain gear. The saddle-bags are absolutely bulging," Alex said.

"Okay. I'll take care of the horses; you go tell your parents we're heading out."

Alex rushed to the house and found them having tea in the den, the family's favorite room. Flames crackled in the huge fieldstone fireplace, whose heavy oak mantel was a masterpiece of Indian craftsmanship. Deeply carved and painted across the edge with tribal symbols and designs, it had been made by a Pueblo artist more than a hundred years ago. The shelf now held aged Navajo baskets and pottery bowls Gramp had collected over the years.

"It's nice and cozy in here, Dad," she said, squeezing his shoulder. "We're ready to go, and Gramp's waiting by the barn."

Her mother smiled at her from a comfortable recliner, where she sat with her feet propped up and a steaming mug in her hands. Alex reached out to gently rub her round stomach and put her ear down to listen.

"Oh, you lucky baby in such a nice, warm, floating world," Alex whispered to the flannel-covered tummy. "I can't wait to hold you." She lifted her head and gave her mom a hug. "Bye, see you later."

"Have fun, honey. I hope you get to see the beavers."

Alex and her dad walked outside arm in arm and met the first pale yellow streak of dawn across the horizon.

"You've been waiting for this a long time," he said. With a grunt he boosted her into the saddle and turned to speak a few quiet words to Gramp.

"Enjoy the trip; be careful. And have a beaver day, Alex," he said with a quick salute.

Chester meandered about a good distance from the dreaded horses. He worked his low-slung body, inchworming up the wide porch steps for a safer view. Nose between the post rails, he fired off rounds of high-pitched barks at Alex.

"Okay, Chettie, you be a good boy! You, too, Goldie!"

15

"Ur-rf!" answered the doxie. Riveted on the scene below, he watched the hoof marks form in the frosty mud when the two moved down the rutted lane.

Their route took them by tumbling streams and along wild animal runs. As they rode, Alex lost herself in Gramp's fascinating stories of the primitive Colorado Indians.

"This is an ancient Ute trail. Prehistoric Amerinds walked these very paths first used by migrating animals. Much later they rode horses the Spaniards brought here from the Old World," he said, slowing James at a fork in the track. A leg signal guided his mount to the right.

"They carved out new passages when they hunted and gathered their food, traded with other tribes, or moved their camps. It's hard to believe that many of the highways across our country today began as Indian foot trails."

Alex had read about the long-ago people. She thought of Indian families packing their belongings for the trek to summer or winter campgrounds. Images of their horses, beautiful rust-colored Appaloosas with spotted rumps, hauling the pole-and-frame carriers called *travois* peppered Alex's imagination.

"Did they stay near here?" she asked.

"Some distance from the ranch there's an immense area called Kenosha Pass. A splendid level plain, it was the place for their summer powwows, and it also served as a winter campground."

"They set up tepees there?"

"Yes. It's cold and snowy in winter but at a much lower elevation than the mountains," Gramp explained. "Old-timers said it was a breathtaking sight from the pass overlook when night fires were burning inside the scores of buffalo-skin dwellings. Their beautiful glow was visible for miles."

"I wish I could have seen that," Alex whispered.

"Me, too. I always loved to hear my parents talk about it."

They were moving through the back country when a chorus of cries broke the quiet. Alex scanned the sky and spotted a flock of

Canada geese flying in their famous wedge formation.

"They're born horn-honkers, all right," Gramp said.

Still curious about the passing wave of talkative geese, Alex tilted her head to catch a final glimpse of them. Her hat flew off as she craned her neck but her chin caught its leather tie.

"I hear the echoes," she said.

On the bank of a boggy creek, they surprised an opossum scratching the dirt for a savory insect. Alex chuckled when she saw his black jellybean-eyes bulge at the strangers passing through his territory.

"You're out late, little man. Why aren't you in bed?" she asked, peering round at him. He just turned his back, nosed open a door under a pile of leaves, and...disappeared.

"He's a magician." Alex cherished her glimpse of the little critter's shy behavior.

The hungry sidekicks stopped for lunch in a high mountain meadow bedecked with wildflowers. Sitting tall on Jessie, Alex inhaled the sweet fragrance of the new-grown grassland.

"It's a giant perfume factory. They love it," she said, pointing at pollen-laden bees. She basked in the midday sun and the gentle breeze that riffled acres of wild iris and Indian paint brush. She smelled the scented clover that grew among lavender-blue sage.

Leaning back and sharing juicy orange slices, they spied a pair of golden eagles soaring free. In effortless flight they rode the warm thermal updrafts far above the mountains.

"Keep an eye on those little jewels over there." Gramp nodded to a host of comical emerald hummingbirds streaking about. Their square-feathered tails created a squeaky whir as they flew. Braking abruptly, they hovered over blossoms, their dainty tongues darting out to sip the nectar.

"Hello, there!" Alex said, trying hard to hold still while a hopeful hummer buzzed in orbit around her scarlet hat.

"I could stay here all day," Alex said. She sneaked a finger out, willing a vivid miniflyer to land on it. No luck.

They carefully packed away the remains of their lunch and

readied their horses. "Jess wants to stay too, Gramp," Alex said. She toed a stone and vowed to come back to this beautiful place. They began their companionable trek across the open rangeland.

"Hey, pardner, come on now. Let's run these horses!" Gramp said. "They need the exercise and so do we!"

Alex rose to the challenge. Her booted heels applied a smart nudge to Jessie's sides. With her long hair flying like a kite tail in the wind, she let out a wild whoop and chased after James and the bouncing gray hat with her grandfather under it.

"Phew!" he said, breathing hard as they arrived at the base of the mountain. Jessie was lathered with sweat when Alex pulled her to a stop.

"Guess I'll enter the next rodeo," she said with a laugh.

"Not a bad idea, gal. You can fly like those eagles."

Saddle leather creaking, they leaned forward to help their horses climb the steep foothills where sunlight sprinkled the glorious quaking aspens, whose light-green leaves, true to their name, jiggled in the afternoon air.

On a steep, narrow trace, a tawny rabbit dashed in front of Jessie. Startled, the usually placid animal sidestepped nervously toward the embankment. Out of normal rhythm, Jess rattled her bridle and chewed her bit. Alex firmed the reins to reassure her.

"Whoa, girl, settle down. You frightened that snowshoe hare more than it scared you." The horse whisked her ears and gave a low nicker through flared nostrils.

"Sh-h-h-h." Alex bent to stroke the silky mane. "Everything's okay now, sweet lady." The ground leveled, and they emerged into a damp, mossy area.

"We're near the pond," Gramp said, drawing up next to Alex. "Let's tether the horses and walk the rest of the way so we don't disturb the beavers."

"Okay. I'll take my bedroll to sit on."

They settled down some distance from the lodge, keeping silent watch. The azure water glistened, unmarred except for a few bugs that dimpled its surface...and they waited. The sun took its own lazy time to shift past an overhanging willow before a dark, polished head appeared and edged toward the bank.

"Probably the father," Gramp whispered.

From deep within, another circle broke the pond's surface. At its center appeared a sleek, sable face. Powerful kicks of its webbed feet propelled a second beaver on its way.

"Now, just wait," Gramp murmured. Moments later, a trio of shiny little noses rose to greet the open air.

"The yearlings," Alex said, "three of them."

Their mother steered a slow turn with her flat tail, taking stock while her youngsters skimmed along, pushing out perfect triple Vs. The two humans savored the private moment of their fellow creatures.

Two more tiny faces emerged with a splash.

"Twins!" Alex whispered. "Maybe it's their first outing." One hand reached out to touch Gramp's arm; the other clamped over her mouth.

Sensing the babies' arrival, the alert mother swam full speed to escort the miniature twosome. Side by side they rushed smoothly toward her through the ripples. Each sleek swimmer greeted the others, and together they performed their very own water ballet.

Gramp and Alex marveled at the wondrous sight before them, Alex's wish come true.

Dusk surrounded the riders as they made their way home. Dad and Chester rose from the porch swing and went to meet them at the barn. When the weary travelers spotted him perched on the fence, Alex had just enough energy left to wave her hat.

"Hi, Dad, we had a great day!"

"I'm glad, honey. I want to hear the whole story." He reached up to help her dismount and steady her shaky legs.

"I can see you're exhausted. Let's get the horses settled."

As Alex brushed down Jess with slow, even strokes, a puzzled frown stole across her forehead. She looked around and paused with her arm in midair. Someone was missing! The brush slipped from her hand and hit the dirt with a dull thud. Alex whirled to face her father.

"Where's Mom?" she asked. Gramp's eyes moved to his son. "She's in the hospital..."

"What happened?" Alex grabbed at his coat sleeve.

"She's fine, honey. The big news is...you have a new baby brother!"

"Mom had our baby! Gramp, did you hear that? I have a brother! Oh, I can't wait to tell my friends. Is Mom all right?" Alex began to pelt him with questions.

"Alex, let your dad talk," Gramp gently reminded her.

"Well, uh, as a matter of fact, Al, you not only have a brother, you have twin brothers," he said, two fingers raised toward the rafters. "All this time we kept it as a surprise for you."

"Wow! Twins!"

Giddy, Alex scooped up Chester and danced him around the barn. Her father grinned, totally understanding her reaction.

"I just remembered something I didn't tell you, Dad. The beavers have brand new twins, too! Just like we do!"

"How about that!"

"So, I think we know two moms who'll really be busy beavers for quite a long time," Gramp said. He kissed Alex and gave his son a hearty handshake that turned into a mighty bear hug.

"Well, I think I know one older kit sister who will be glad to help," Alexandra mimicked with a grin. She ducked between them and popped up, centered firmly in her own family circle.

The Rusty Village

A storm raged above the graystone ranch house that evening. Gusts of wind rattled the wooden shutters, and shafts of lightning flashed beyond the windows of the upstairs bedroom. The two girls clamped their hands over their ears, waiting for the following waves of thunderous sound to roll by.

Alex's best friend peeked out from her place of honor in the top bunk. "Another storm, phooey!" Alexandra chuckled at Skylyn's reaction and joined her to peer through the kaleidoscope of raindrops on the glass.

"Maybe it will clear by morning...let's hope," she said.

"It better, or we can't go to the old mine."

Skylyn Eaglefeather was visiting for the weekend, and Alex and her grandfather had planned a hike to the mountain site of an abandoned silver-mining town. Much too excited to sleep, the girls talked late into the night.

"Wake up!" Skylyn leaned down and shook Alex just as the alarm clanged.

21

"Huh?" Alex blustered as she gave the off button a mighty slap. The clock rocketed off the nightstand and landed with a clank. She heaved a sigh and flopped back on the pillow.

"It's still raining, Al." Sky worried at her bottom lip and moved to the head of the bed to look outside for the hundredth time.

"Oh, don't worry; it might just be coming from the roof. We'll let Gramp decide," she said.

The dark brown Jeep sat out front packed and waiting, while Gramp studied a map.

"How long will it take?" Alex asked, tossing her hat into the back seat.

"We'll drive about an hour, and then it depends how fast you gals want to walk."

"I hope we'll have time to see everything," she replied.

"Me, too, Gramp!" Sky said with an impish grin. Their laughter brought Alex's parents out of the house, each toting a twin bundled in a blue blanket.

"You look raring to go," her mother said, holding Chandler so they could pat the blond baby and stroke his soft pink cheeks.

"We're ready," they answered after giving Tyler equal attention.

"Your grandfather and I explored the area years ago. We had a great time, so I know you're in for a real treat," her dad said as he tipped a bottle to his son's mouth.

"I'll miss the little ones," Alex said, her eyes intent on the babies as they guzzled their milk.

"I know, honey, but your brothers will snooze all day. So go and enjoy."

With Goldie nipping at his heels, Chester hurried to Alexandra and wiped his muddy paws down her jeans. The young retriever followed her friend and slowly circled them, wagging her creamy tail.

"What have you two been doing? Did you sneak into the stable to pester the cats?" She gave the doxie a scratch. He rolled onto his back, wiggled his legs in the air, and begged for more. Goldie demanded her turn.

"I know, sweetie, you need lots of love, just like my little brothers."

Their four-wheel drive bounced along muddy lanes while Gramp hunted for a good place to park. The girls grabbed the overhead handles whenever the Jeep hit a deep rut that snapped their heads back.

"It's like a bucking bronc!" Skylyn cried out.

As soon as Gramp pulled to a stop they perched on the tailgate to lace leather hiking boots and strap on backpacks for the long trek to the mine.

"You'll need your rain gear; the trees are still dripping," said Gramp. "Okay, let's go! We're gonna have fun!"

"Onward, Gramp, you're our guide for today." Alex called as they ducked under moisture-laden branches the sun would soon blot dry. He lead them through a grove of aspens with green splotches of lichen camouflaging their creamy bark. Hiking uphill at a steady pace, they soon stepped out of the heavy woods onto a comfortable, wide trail. By now the clouds had cleared, and they could pack away their ponchos.

Skylyn jiggled an overhanging fir branch just as Alexandra walked under it.

"Plink! You're all wet!"

"Spf-f-zft! I'll get even! You wait!"

"Just look at that! There's a squirrel leading our parade." With a twinkle in her eye Skylyn pointed it out. Looking for its mate, the little creature raced ahead of them up the ancient buffalo trail. It launched itself at a tree trunk and spiraled up the rough bark. Seated on a high limb, it chittered loudly with its quivering, question-mark tail punctuating each syllable.

"That's the end of his story—see his telltale mark?" Gramp chuckled as he paused to lean on his hiking stick. The girls groaned at his joke and clanked their sticks against his like dueling swords.

Wandering off the trail, they slid down a slope toward a rock-strewn creek and stopped to rest on a boulder.

"I wonder how the Indians and settlers got across big creeks and rivers," Alex said.

"My grandmother told me it was very dangerous," Skylyn was the first to answer.

"Yes, it was hazardous without all the equipment we have today," Gramp confirmed.

"My dad says our Navajo and Ute ancestors studied a problem and then worked to solve it," Sky said, "just the way we do our math in school."

"You're right," he said. "They looked for shallow areas to ford, and eventually such places became well known. The Indians learned to investigate their land, cooperate with nature, and pass their findings along to others. Homesteaders who journeyed west in the mideighteen hundreds found they could follow the same trails and passages."

"The Oregon and the Santa Fe trails are two I know about; but settlers traveling over them had a hard time," Alex recalled. "Whole families left their homes and rode away in canvas-covered wagons pulled by teams of horses or oxen."

"And before they climbed into the mountains," Gramp added, "they had to discard most of their belongings to make their prairie schooners lighter. Everyone got behind to push. The animals were often so exhausted from months on the march that the people ended up walking alongside them most of the way."

"I know about that! I saw an old picture of a beautiful piano and its bench sitting in the middle of the prairie. It looked so lonely," Alex said.

"They came for gold and found unbelievable hardship," Gramp nodded. "Many turned back, got sick, or had accidents and died. Thousands of graves with hastily made markers bordered the trails."

"That's sad when they had such high hopes," Alex said quietly.

"One part of the Oregon Trail called Limestone Pass is still visible in southeast Wyoming," Gramp continued. "It shows deep wagon-wheel scrapes that wore ridges into the boulders from all the caravans fighting their way over the mountain."

"I think you'd both like the huge rock wall called Register Cliff. It's near that same pass and is covered with names and dates. You can still read signatures carved in the stone by the pioneers and their wagon masters who made that terrible odyssey. Newcomers always looked to see if their friends had made it that far; then they too inscribed their names and dates. It became an important 'newspaper' and gave them courage to go on." The girls sat quietly as they drank their cold juice and pondered his story.

"I bet we can cross this stream," Alex said, roused from her thoughts.

"How would you do it?" Gramp asked.

"I'd look for a place where some stones are showing above water and use my stick to help me along, rock by rock."

"That's an idea. What do you think, Skylyn?"

"It's good, but I'd look for fallen trees to walk on. Mr. Tanner, do you think we could try?"

"Yes, let's, Gramp," Alex begged.

"Okay, you've sweet-talked me into it. We'll follow the stream and see what we find. There's a shortcut to the mine on the other side, but we have to be very careful, gals," he cautioned.

Sun glistened on the rushing water as they worked their way along the bank. In the distance they saw a plump gray bird dive under the water, only to surface upstream a short time later.

"What is it?" Alex asked. Her grandfather reached into the pocket of his canvas vest for a small book and passed it over to her.

"Look it up," he challenged. She knelt on the grass and flipped the pages.

"American dipper," she reported.

"He's a dipper for sure. He must hold his nose to do that!" Skylyn observed. Everyone laughed at the thought.

"Dippers search the bottom for fish and insect larvae," she read aloud. They watched as it automatically dipped its body as it teetered on a rock and eyed the watery depths, again ready to plunge in and swim against the current to hunt for lunch.

The hikers continued searching for a natural bridge. They were trampling along the mushy shore when Gramp pointed to the opposite side.

"Look over there; it's a muskrat," he whispered.

A small, light-brown animal worked his way along the margins of the stream, looking for berries, twigs, and other succulent bits of vegetation. He turned back and dove to his underground burrow in the bank.

"Muskrat fur was like money to trappers. They set snares for them as well as bears, wolves, and foxes. At trading posts they bartered pelts for food and supplies," Gramp said. "Some species, like the beaver, were almost wiped out."

"Ugh! I can't think about those poor animals trapped in steel jaws. It makes me feel awful!" Alex complained.

"Today, thank goodness, strict limits for taking fish and game help a great deal."

"I've heard on TV that the American eagle and the peregrine falcons are off of the endangered species list. Isn't that great!" Alex said.

"It's wonderful!" they agreed.

"I'd like to be a park ranger when I grow up so I can watch over wildlife and the land." Alex spread her arms to encompass the beauty all around them. "I especially love the fir trees. I don't ever want to see them cut down. The animals need them!"

"My grandfather and his family tied strips of colored cloth to branches to send their prayers blowing in the wind and to help them discover their guardian spirits," Skylyn said. Her gaze riveted on her best friend as she listened to her dreams.

At last they found steppingstones crossing the stream. Gramp walked right behind Skylyn as she went over and returned to guide Alex.

"Look!" Poised before her last step, Sky turned, and Alex plunged her stick into the water with a loud plop. "I win!" She giggled as she scrambled past.

"Just wait!" Skylyn warned. She slapped her pole splat! into the cold mountain stream. The shower missed its intended target and caught Gramp full in the face! His spits and sputters drew gales of laughter from the two girls.

None the worse, they scampered over the rocky shore and clambered up the slick, grassy slope.

"We did it! We're strong and brave!" they exclaimed, waving their sticks in the air.

"You are also wise and inventive," Gramp declared. "You found a ford, and now we don't have to make a lengthy detour."

"I'm glad we don't have a canoe, or we'd have to carry it on our shoulders like the Indians did." Alex turned slowly toward her grandfather.

"Oh dear! That means another trip, I suppose," he said, with an exaggerated sigh.

"A canoe trip! That would be super," Alex said. Gramp clapped a hand to his forehead.

Moving away from the creek and into a thicket, they soon found a small clearing scattered with stumps. Alex placed two hands on top of one and hopped over it to land on both feet with a muffled thump. Skylyn caught on and bounded over another to catch up with her leaping friend. They stopped to look skyward when they heard the piercing shriek of a red-tailed hawk as it pounced upon a dove in midair. When the hawk swooped away, it neatly shifted the catch in its claws to carry it lengthwise.

"Why did he do that?" they asked.

"It makes it easier to fly; the wind doesn't push against it as much."

"I feel bad for the poor bird," Alex said, true to form, "but I know bigger birds feed their babies with smaller prey."

"It's called a cycle. Remember, Alex? We read about it in earth science," Skylyn said.

"Uh-huh, the food chain."

"Your teachers would be so proud of you!" Gramp said.

They stopped for lunch in a sunny glade. The girls examined some fallen logs and marveled at the way dead trees provide food and shelter for forest insects, plants, and small animals.

"There's bracket fungus," Alex said. She pointed out the tan "shelves" growing on a live tree as well as a dead one. "Chipmunks and pikas could have a tea party on them."

"The decaying logs are creating new soil, and beetles and ants love that. See the mosses and ferns taking root all over them?" Sky said.

"Maybe we could make a terrarium when we get back. That would be fun. We have lots of good dirt and plants by the barn."

As they neared the old mine, Gramp told them to look for signs of silver in the rocks.

"I see a lot of bottle caps," Sky said, "some old but others are new."

"That's litter!" Alex intoned. "People just haven't learned that you carry out of the forest what you carry in!"

They walked through a stand of cottonwood trees whose large seed puffs covered the ground in a white carpet. Sky and Alex helped the breeze distribute them, shouting "Pillow fight! Pillow fight!"

Before long they came to a clearing strewn with rusted machinery. It also contained a few small dwellings in various stages of collapse.

"This is it! We're here!"

"Wow! It's neat!" Skylyn said to Gramp as he emerged from the wood.

"Glad you approve!" he answered. "Now, move carefully, and watch out for mining holes! They should all be filled in, but you never know."

Everywhere they turned Sky and Alex discovered curiosities to investigate.

"Look there," Skylyn said to no one in particular. "It's a railroad track." Alex came running.

"I found a car with a top that tilts. Come and see it, Gramp."

"That's a part of the narrow-gauge rail system the miners used. It's called an ore cart. Workers loaded it with rock, and mules walking between the rails hauled it to the surface. Outside they tipped the car to dump the load. Later on it was sorted and checked for silver."

The girls explored dilapidated houses and poked their heads into the broken doorways of roofless, tumbled-down shanties.

"Here's the site of a former shack. You can see its outline," Alex said as her boots traced the edge of the aged foundation. "That stone fireplace must have been well built to last so long. They probably cooked on it, too."

"You're right about that," Gramp told them from where he sat watching on a nearby rise. "The foundation is usually the strongest part of a house, so it lasts the longest. The planks on the sides and roof have long since rotted away. A house is somewhat like your favorite fir tree, Alex. With good care it will grow sturdy enough to survive harsh weather and live a long life."

"Gramp, you said that in such a nice way; I understand perfectly! That's neat."

"Me too!" Sky chimed in.

"Okay, my young miners, I think there's a dump site right here under our feet. I see fragments of broken bottles and some tin cans and several handmade nails." For the next hour the girls poked around in search of further artifacts. They set off up a low man-made hill to go see the covered mines.

"This is a filled-in mine that still bears traces of silver," Gramp said. "See there? Those dark trails leading from the shaft are called *tailings*. Gold mines have yellow tails."

"Here's a rock with something shiny in it," Skylyn said. Gramp pronounced it precious metal, delighting Sky. Alexandra found another and gave a shout.

"Look! I can scratch off little flecks with my fingernail. That is so cool! Real silver nailpolish!"

"You've hit the mother lode, Alex!" he said.

There were other hillocks that once contained shafts but were now overgrown with vines and wildflowers.

"Most everything again becomes part of nature," Gramp said with reverance.

"I'm glad," Skylyn replied.

Alex meandered away, prospecting on her own. She dug out a worn mule shoe, a broken machine handle, and some pottery shards. Pretending to be an old-time miner, she pictured herself with smudges of dirt on her face, a scraggly beard, and a big felt hat. In her mind she led a string of long-eared mules over rugged mountain passes. Picks, shovels, and other supplies stuck out of large baskets strapped tightly to their sides.

Suddenly she stepped into a crumbling hole that had been hidden by a thick growth of weeds. Surface gravel and sandy soil poured in around her feet and sucked her down. She pushed against the ground and tried to pull back, but nothing happened—her legs were trapped tight in a pit that tried to swallow her each time she moved.

"Help!" Alex cried as she grabbed an exposed root and frantically brushed away ants that nipped as they scrambled over her, fleeing their broken nest.

Seated on a piece of fallen timber, Gramp was telling Skylyn about mining machinery. He lifted his head to listen intently and looked around for Alex. Where was she?

"Help!" came the distant cry. He jumped up in alarm.

"Yell louder so we can locate you!" he commanded as he ran toward the faint sound of her voice. Skylyn was faster. She hurtled to the bottom of the hill. "Alex!" she screamed as she ran. "Where are you?"

"Over here!" Alex hollered back, continuing to writhe in the deepening hole. The rescuers ran, thrashing through the tall grass and clambering over piles of dirt.

"Wave your arms!" Gramp instructed, following Skylyn.

Alex waved once but had to grab the root again when more

earth slid inward to tighten its grip on her waist. She continued to call, now trying to remain motionless.

"There she is—by that tree!" Skylyn was the first to spot her. She signaled wildly and threw herself flat on the ground near Alex. "I've got her arm, but I can't budge her!"

"Hold on!" Gramp said as he raced up. He grasped Alex under the armpits and tugged hard. Sky dug at the soil entrapping her. At last the greedy pit released its hold, and she was free.

"Alexandra!" Gramp gasped with a wobbly grin. "You'll turn my hair snow white yet!"

"It was awful," Alex said, as she hugged him tight. "I don't know what happened. I was walking along, searching for stuff, and my foot went in the hole. The rest of me just followed."

He returned her squeeze while Skylyn dusted off the dirt and homeless ants.

"It's a deserted prairie dog mound, honey. It's not deep like a mine shaft, but the recent rains have made it close in on itself. You got caught in it." With a shaky arm he wiped his wet brow. "An accident like this is the most important reason to always go hiking with a buddy." It was a lesson they wouldn't forget.

"Girls," Gramp said from behind the wheel, "we'll stop at Buena Vista to eat before we get home. I'm sure Alex's parents have had dinner and are busy getting the twins to bed."

"Jeepers! I never get time to play with my brothers; all they ever do is sleep," Alex grumbled. The other two laughed at her griping.

"Mr. Tanner, what is 'Beena Veesta' or however you pronounce it?" Sky asked.

"It's a town at the foot of the mountain. Before we go down we'll pull over so you can look around." A few minutes later they swung their tired legs out of the Jeep and gasped in awe at the scene below.

"It's beautiful!" Alex turned in circles to get a full view of the mountains.

"Why are you laughing, Gramp?" she asked in puzzlement.

"So you like it, huh? Well, my dears, Buena vista is Spanish for..."

"Beautiful view!" they finished for him.

"Bwena veesta!" the girls chanted all the way to town, amusing Gramp as he drove.

The travelers bought their dinner and carried it to a picnic table next to the busy Arkansas River. They watched a noisy group of rafters get out of their vans parked next to the truck that hauled their huge rubber boats.

"Rafting! Now that would be a great..."

"Don't even think it!" Gramp muttered, shaking his head. "Nope! That's your father's trip to take with you when you're older!" he declared with Skylyn following their good-natured banter.

Asking Gramp to wait, the girls returned to the small country store. They soon emerged, each carrying a large bag.

"That smells great!" Gramp said. He took a deep breath and pointed the Jeep toward the highway and home. When the dusty vehicle with its snoozing passengers pulled up beneath lighted windows, Alex's dad heard the motor and came out to greet them.

"Welcome back," he said, shaking his father's hand.

"Hi, Dad. Are the boys in blue asleep?" Alex asked, getting out as fast as her tired body would move.

"Yes, honey. Did you have fun?" he asked, chuckling at this daughter's question. He went to help unload the Jeep.

"I'll take our gear, son; you get these weary hikers inside," Gramp said, urging them toward the house.

Gramp joined them for breakfast the next morning just as Alex clinked a spoon on her empty juice glass.

"Everyone is invited to a special ceremony in the back yard in about ten minutes."

Her curious family arrived to find an old blanket clipped on a rope that stretched between a tree limb and the fence. Chester and Goldie tumbled over one another in a rush to check behind the strange object hanging in the garden.

Alex's mom took a seat on the swing. Dad and Gramp handed her the twins, and she gently set it in motion with a push of her foot. Skylyn leaned against the tree and summoned the dogs to join her.

The men relaxed in lawn chairs as Alex climbed on a large stone.

"Dad, Mom, and the little munchkins. I learned a lot with Gramp and Skylyn yesterday. I've been thinking hard about a gift for you. I think I found the perfect present to go with my prayers for my brothers to grow strong and tall and have a long life."

Alex turned and nodded to Sky, who hurried to untie the rope. The coverlet dropped to reveal two small, Colorado blue spruce trees planted side by side in the rock garden. Bright bands of cloth and some tiny feathers tied on their branches gaily fluttered in the warm air. "I bought them with the allowance I earned cleaning the stables," she said.

Her father hugged Alex for her thoughtfulness, and she returned to the swing just in time to see Tyler put his thumb in his mouth. Chandler blinked drowsily at his big sister and slowly closed his eyes.

Skylyn declared that the new plantings would one day become a Buena Vista. Alexandra reached out to embrace the twins and her delighted mother.

"Well, right now," she said, "I think this is the most beautiful view in the whole wide world."

It All Started with a Song

They're quiet, but they seem okay. What's going on? Alex wondered. Whenever we go to the mailbox, they're usually determined to have a rattle-and-roll ride.

"Run fast!" Tyler demanded from the front seat of the stroller.

"We are fast!" said Chandler in the rumble seat. He promptly grabbed his rubber bat and bopped his brother on the head. Arms, legs, elbows, and fists exploded.

"Ow!" the injured Tyler cried with large tears gathering on his cheeks. He recovered quickly when he realized that a few good stomps on the metal footrest sounded very much like a small cattle stampede.

"I'm going as fast as I can, and I am hitting all the bumps! Do you think this is the wild mouse ride at the fair? Well, it's not!" Alexandra ground out through clenched teeth. She tried counting to ten, but it didn't help.

"Look," she pointed out, "there's the magpie you like. He's following us again." The large bird lowered his iridescent wings and spread his long tail in a gentle landing on the nearby sagebrush.

"Pie," both murmured, waving to their black-and-white friend, who, in turn sat tall and eyed the trio.

"Maaag," he chirruped.

"He's looking for a handout," she whispered to the boys. "Sorry, we don't have any scraps for you this morning." The bird tagged along until Alex stopped to check for mail and snatch a well-deserved rest.

"Go!" the twins roared, shaking the stroller.

"Okay, where to now?"

"Mickey!" they shouted in unison.

"We'll visit Mick, but don't think I'm pushin' this contraption to Disney World, because I'm not!"

The Shetland pony came over and stuck his head between the rails to nuzzle their palms. The boys liked the velvety feel of his soft nose and giggled happily at his fuzzy whiskers.

"Here comes Wrangler Rob, boys," Alex said. They greeted their favorite ranch hand.

"Hi!" he said and hunkered down to chat. "You boys are growing by leaps and bounds! I'm told there was a birthday celebrated here when I was on vacation. Pretty soon you'll be practicing barrel racing with me just like your big sister!" Their wide-eyed gaze never left Rob's face and his battered cowboy hat.

"What's next, guys?" Rob asked.

"Cat!" they sang out.

"Forward march!" Rob said, pointing to the barn.

Momma cat and Alex trusted the boys to carefully lift the kittens from the new litter. They sat cross-legged on a fragrant bale of hay with a calico furball nestled cozily in each lap.

"They're just tiny babies. They're only six days old. See?" she pointed out, "Their eyes are still closed, but they'll open in about four more days."

"We're two!" Chandler patted his chest and reached over to touch Tyler's.

"Yes, you're both two years old now." They stayed with the

kittens for a while and then moved to the corral to greet other animals. Jessie was very willing to have little visitors offering delicious red-apple treats. When the brothers grew quiet, Alex took a peek under the stroller's canopy.

"Ah, at last," she murmured and wheeled them past the house to the back yard. She found a quiet place under a tree and gently rocked the sleeping twins.

As Alex eased back against the rough bark of the trunk, she saw Kiki, the family's beloved tomcat that just happened to have a feminine name. He was sitting on a broken board once part of the bird feeder Gramp had nailed on a fence post. The cat slowly switched his coal black tail and purred. He seemed content for the moment; but whenever he settled there, a loud songfest usually erupted nearby. She searched for the mockingbird, a proud father-to-be. Sure enough, she spotted him perched on his customary branch.

"Are you keeping watch over that outrageous pair?" Gramp asked, slipping into his old lawn chair.

"We have the best seats in the house," she said, "but I think the twins are going to miss the show." She nodded toward the fence as the cat lowered his head for a snooze.

"I wonder if Kiki will try to get even with that bird," she mused.

"I don't know." Gramp shook his head. "But I think he'll be lucky to get out alive!"

"Who—the cat or the bird?" she teased.

"We'll just have to wait and see," he said with a wink. The bird was getting ready to boast: he puffed out his feathered breast and began a lengthy trill.

Kiki awoke in midsnore and automatically issued a swat at the bothersome mocker. Though he missed his target by a mile, the momentum of the move sent the groggy cat toppling from the fence! For a split second Kiki, too, became airborne.

Gramp whooped. Alexandra jumped up and shouted, "Hooray! Poppa's safe until the next go-round!"

Startled, Chandler and Tyler woke with a yowl.

"Sorry, guys." She tried to soothe them but gave up and headed for the house, the twins squawking the whole way. When their mother heard the racket and came to grab Tyler, Chester spied the cat and was out in a flash. The first half of Chet cleared the top step. His second half had no chance to land before the riled warbler attacked! It dive-bombed the doxie's head, his most vulnerable part.

"Yelp!" Chester cried at a glancing blow right above his eye. His backside hit the ground, and he shot away like a rocket.

Kiki, rebounding from his fall, gathered up the remainder of his eight lives, snarled at Chet when he zipped past, and decided to join in the free-for-all. The feisty bird kept up the barrage. He zapped the cat on the ear, sending the frantic feline into a perfect backflip before making a running dive under the shed. From then on it was all-out war. Everyone froze on the spot, but the twins were the first to react. They wriggled in their mother's protective arms.

"Get down!" they protested.

"Not with that three-ring circus going on, you're not!" she answered. Gales of laughter shook Alex as she turned back to the ruckus.

"Now's your chance, Chet!" she called, summoning him with wild hand signals. The dog bounded up the steps and plunged inside.

"You're safe, little one," Alex said. Chester headed straight to his water dish for a long, cool drink and then to his soft rug for a well-deserved rest.

They finally got the boys settled down to play, and Alex helped prepare lunch. Gramp peeked through the screen. "Let's eat outside, ladies; it's too nice to stay in." He went in to gather paper plates and cups and headed out to the picnic table with the twins in tow. He kept the boys busy until Alex arrived to set the table and pour their drinks.

Chandler clapped when he saw his mom carrying out the food with Chester close beside her, his brown nose twitching at the tantalizing aroma of meat. She set out a platter piled high with sandwiches just as Chandler knocked over his cup.

"Never mind, I brought a towel," Anne said and briskly pulled it out of her apron pocket. She moved the large platter to the bench and mopped the spill. Alex tied a clean bib on her brother and refilled his lemonade.

Gramp handed each a plate just as the mockingbird began another peppy serenade.

"Oh no, not again!" Alex cried, peering into the trees.

"Dog!" tattled Chandler, pointing to the tray.

"He sure is at it again! Shoo! Get away!" The culprit sped off with a sandwich in his mouth and their mother in hot pursuit.

Ty and Chandler nodded to each other and for once agreed. "Bad dog."

"Add the cat to that mixture, and Chettie could be in big trouble," Gramp said, wiping his eyes.

"Uh-oh! Look over there." Alex stood up to get a better view. The cat squeezed out from beneath the shed, and set off after the runners.

"Kiki's joined the race for the bologna and cheese!" Alex announced, hopping onto the bench to call the comical contest. "All three are hurtling along the hedge! Mom's gaining on Chet, and the mocker's bearing down on the cat!"

"It's a good thing Goldilocks is with your dad, or it would be total chaos," Gramp said, shaking his head in disbelief. Moments later the bird was back on his branch, carefully preening his ruffled feathers.

"How much longer until the eggs hatch?" Alex asked.

"About two more weeks or so," he replied, "if Mr. Mocker can keep up the defense against his four-legged neighbors."

"I think those birds should find another place to raise their family," Alex said.

"What they need is a realtor," Gramp added.

"House," muttered Chan, as Chester was put in the kitchen.

"Now that's a great idea," his sister said.

"What is?" Gramp scratched his head.

"We can make a new house for them. I'll be their agent," she kidded. "How much should I charge?"

"After all the entertainment, that house should be for rent for a song!"

"Sing," Chan said and smiled at his mother's arrival.

"I'll sing to you after I've eaten," she said. She sighed and slowly lowered herself onto the bench.

"No more music today, please," Gramp pleaded, rolling his eyes.

She only shrugged and sipped her lemonade.

"Hi, lunch bunch!" called Dad as he sauntered through the gate. "What's all the commotion about? Goldie wouldn't come near the yard, not even for food."

"Well, Dad," said Alex, "it all started with a song..."

"What's that mean?" He moved around the table piling food on his plate. "This looks good; I'm starving. How are the boys in blue doing?" he asked, finally settling down.

"Blue," Tyler said and looked down to check his shirt.

"Red!" Chandler proclaimed and pulled his T-shirt out of his shorts. He made a terrible face.

Mom propped her elbows on the table, cupped her forehead in her hands and groaned.

"Don't look at me!" replied Gramp.

"Still eating!" Dad said with his mouth quite full.

"I am not on diaper duty!" dclared Alexandra, "and we have to make a birdhouse. Come on, Gramp!"

"Red!" Chandler shouted again, caught up in all the fun.

Alex stopped and looked back at her grandfather. "Now that's another good idea..."

"We'll paint it red!" Gramp bellowed, both hands waving her on as they scurried off to the toolshed.

Grandma's Troubles

"I don't want to go! I hate it!" Alexandra shouted with her overloaded emotions bouncing into each other. Slamming the diaper bag into the rear of the Jeep, she threw her sweater on top, and stormed away.

"Alexandra! We're ready! Where is she, Steven?" her mother asked.

"She passed me when I went back to get the car seats," he said, working to secure them.

"Anne," Gramp offered, "the twins and I will look around the barn. You want to check the house?"

She hurried down the path. Stepping into the foyer, she called again. There was no answer. Where could that girl be? As she headed for the stairs a sound from the family room made her turn.

"Alex, are you in there?" Tiptoeing toward a wingchair, she peeked over the back and found her oldest child with her legs curled beneath her and her face jammed into an upholstered corner. Her body quivered with sobs.

"What's the matter, dear heart?" her mother asked. She edged her hip onto the seat and gathered her close. Alex hiccuped and pressed her cheek against her mother's chest, beginning a new round of tears.

"You're having problems about seeing Grandma, aren't you?" With a long, drawn-out sigh, Alex bobbed her head.

"Sweetie, I thought you were okay after we talked about it. Tell me what's upset you. I'm sure Gramp and Dad will find plenty to keep the boys busy." Alex held her mother tight and whimpered.

"Are you frightened of seeing Grandma sick?"

"Yes," she whispered.

"What exactly are you worried about?" she coaxed and felt the slight shrug of Alex's shoulders. Her fingers stroked away the tension.

"Remember when I mentioned that all patients in a restorative-nursing home are someone's mother, father, or beloved family member like your grandma?" Alex looked up as she continued. "Medical care can be given much more easily there, honey, better than in their own homes."

"I don't know what scares me—maybe it's because I can't picture what that place is like."

"You know what? It's more like a college dormitory—remember visiting your cousin at the University of Colorado?"

"Uh-huh," Alex answered. She sat up straighter. "Jan had a big room with two beds, and another girl lived there too."

"Same for Gram—she's in a big room with pretty curtains at the window, and she has a roommate named Elizabeth, a nice woman with a great sense of humor. She's very good with your grandma. You'll like her."

"We've talked about all that ever since her fall," Alex said, nodding. "I still can't explain what bothers me."

"Would you rather stay here with Dad?"

"No, I miss Gram. I want to see her and take her the new TV, but..." Alex flopped back against the soft cushion as fresh teardrops pooled in her eyes and slid down her cheeks. Once again her mother drew her into the safe haven of her arms.

"I don't want to see her hurting. I just couldn't stand it!" Her voice rose higher. She reached for another tissue and buried her nose in it.

"Oh, honey, she's doing fine. Her operation was a success, and the doctor says she'll be fit as a fiddle in no time. The fractured hip is mending nicely, and she has aides to help her day and night."

"What if she won't be able to walk again? Then we can't go to the bridge to find chipmunks, or to skip stones when we sit on the rocks." She released all the questions that had been gnawing at her.

"The doctor assures me she's in good health. She's not that old, you know. As soon as she can get around well enough, she'll come home with us for the rest of her recovery. I know exactly how you feel—you want her to be whole again and so do I."

"Yes! I just want her to be the same Grandma I've always had," she said.

"She will be. She's beginning physical therapy, but it..."

"Will it hurt?"

"No, it will help her. It's like a massage. You know how we rub Dad's shoulders when he's awfully tired and how I work the cramps from too much riding out of your legs?"

"It makes my muscles relax."

"Okay, that's what her therapists are doing. They knead her legs and move her muscles for her and encourage her to do stretching exercises on her own. They want her strong so they can teach her to walk again."

"She'll have to learn to walk again? Just like the twins!" she said with a squeak. Her mother nodded and rose from the chair with a twinkle in her eye.

"We'll get Chan and Ty to show her how to take the first steps. How about that?"

"Hah!" Alex replied, needing to laugh. "I can't see Gram crawling first, though; I think the boys would hop on her back for a ride before we could catch them."

"She'll have a walker for support. You'll see when you get there." Her mom chuckled.

Alexandra unfolded her legs and stood up to give her a hug and a smile.

"I'm ready now. Thanks for helping me understand a little better. I'm still a bit scared, but I want to go."

"I felt the same way when I went to check out the home before the hospital transferred her there," she said as she threaded her arm through Alex's. "Now, don't you think we'd better get out there and free the men from the twins' clutches?" her mom suggested as they made their way through the house. "Gram's been asking for you and your brothers. I'm sure seeing you will be the best therapy for her."

"Don't count on it. You haven't seen the twins in action since you've been going to the home every day."

"What have they been up to?" Alex gave her a running account of their exploits.

They found the gentlemen seated on the fence by the barn, each holding a twin. Dad signaled for silence. They edged closer and leaned against a post to wait. A brown mouse poked its whiskered snout from under a loose board and skittered out to steal a few pieces of cracked corn missed by the free-roaming hens.

"Cat!" Chandler sounded the alarm when one of the barnyard felines stealthily crept toward it. His father was quick to reassure him that by then the brave mouse was safely back in its nest, sharing breakfast with its family.

"Well, that's that for the mouse patrol today, boys," he said. "We'll visit the new momma goat and her kid when you come home this afternoon."

"Ladies, I'm chauffeur of the day, so I'm all yours. Shall we proceed while I still have the strength?" Gramp ruffled Alex's hair.

"Alex," Gramp asked while unloading the stroller, "will you help me with the TV? There's probably a cart around somewhere we can use."

"Okay, and I've a present for Gram, too," Alex said. Feeling her stomach knot, she rubbed it to help relieve the pain pinching her insides.

"You can push the boys for me, honey. I've got the clean clothes to carry," her mother said. She watched from the car door as Alex undid Ty's seat belt and climbed out.

They saw the flag flapping in the breeze on a pole that rose from the middle of a circular garden filled with red, white, and blue flowers, a cheerful reminder that it was nearly the Fourth of July. Drawing to a stop, Alex folded her arms across her stomach, hunched her shoulders, and waited for the rest to catch up. She noticed the people seated on the long verandah, most of them in wheelchairs, some on beautiful white wicker settees.

An elderly gentlemen wheeled himself off of the porch and down the ramp to the sidewalk.

"What have we here? Am I seeing double?" he asked.

"Twins," Alex responded and smiled at him.

"Hello, Ed! I see you've met my children," their mother said.

"Anne, good to see you. So this is the rest of the family. Visiting your mother again?"

"Yes, and I'd like you to meet Robert Tanner, Steven's father, better known to all as Gramp," she said when he joined the group.

"Have a wonderful visit, folks," Ed said with a salute. He set his chair in motion and rolled on down the walk.

The twins were looking right and left at all the gray-haired ladies who resembled their grandma. Someone held the door, and they entered a large peach-and-blue foyer where patients chatted with friends and relatives. Some napped in their chairs.

"Oh, they're adorable. I have twin girls, but they're grown women now," said a lady seated alone just inside the doorway. "They're beautiful, just like you." She reached out to Alexandra.

"Thank you," she replied, slipping her hand into the gnarled one.

"Will you adjust my footrest for me, honey? It's caught up, and I'm not at all comfortable."

"Sure," Alex said. She knelt down to give the little platform a push and heard the click that locked it into place.

"Try that," she encouraged, her hands guiding the quilted slippers into place.

"It's perfect. Thank you, sweetie," she said, beaming up at her newfound helper. They continued to chat while Alex gently smoothed the pink coverlet over her lap. Gramp and her mom waited nearby with smiles on their faces.

"Room 213," her mother said, breezing past Alex, who was busy checking the brass nameplates beside each door. "This way; it's the last one on the left, next to the emergency exit." The boys looked into each open room as they passed and waved to the occupants.

"Come in." A familiar voice answered their knock.

"Surprise! You've got lots of visitors today," Anne greeted her mother and stepped aside.

"How wonderful! Welcome," Grandma said. She pushed a button to move the top half of her bed upright and called for hugs all around.

"Hi, Gram. How are you?" Alex said when it was her turn. She touched her grandma's cheeks with both hands. "You look so nice, and your hair is beautiful."

"Thank you. I just got it washed and set. Then I came back here for a short nap," she said.

"Where did you get it done?" Alex asked, looking puzzled.

"There's a salon in the next wing. The stylist comes for me, and someone brings me back afterwards. Next time I'll get my nails done, too."

"That's neat," Alex said. "I didn't know they had a hairdresser."

"Lots of good stuff goes on here. It's a busy place. There's a hobby room for anyone interested in pottery or painting and an activities room for games and social events. We can even vote right here at election time! You'll have to take the grand tour."

"Chandler and Tyler, come and see Grandma!" Anne set the boys carefully on each side of the bed.

"Are you better yet?" Tyler asked.

"I'm fine and I'll be walking soon; just bet on it, Ty."

"That chair goes," Chandler said. Now familiar with wheelchairs, he spotted hers parked in the corner near her bed.

"You're right, and I can speed in it," she said. "Do you want a ride in my car?" she whispered to them.

"Mother, I don't think so," Anne said with a worried frown.

"They'll be fine. Gramp can push them," she said. Before he got the chair unfolded, Chandler slid off the bed and danced his way out into the hall. He spotted the exit door and pushed on its long bar, promptly setting off a shrill alarm.

"Oh, no!" Anne cried. She ran out to snatch him away, and gestured to a nurse hurrying toward them that everything was all right. She explained the racket to the twins while the rest of them tried to hide their amusement.

"All right. You gals visit, and I'll push the future Indy 500 racers around," Gramp volunteered.

"Here's my roommate," Grandma said. Elizabeth came in, rolling her walker forward with each step.

"Alexandra, I'm glad to meet you. I saw your grandfather and met your little brothers," Elizabeth said, maneuvering her way to the far side of the room. "I've heard all about you. I'd like to show you my family. I have a wonderful granddaughter your age." She got out her photo album.

Later, when her mother went for coffee, Alex straightened her grandma's covers, watered the plants, and sorted the mail.

"Anything else I can do?" she asked, sitting down beside her.

"Just having you here is enough, sweetie. I'm so glad you came," she answered. Her loving smile included her daughter, who appeared with cups of steaming coffee for the women.

Gramp soon returned with the boys. They hopped out of the chair to check out the spokes on its big wheels and the handbrakes.

"What did you do?"

"Played bingo," Tyler announced.

"We went to the activities room," Gramp said. "I pushed them up to the game table next to one of the residents. They scooped up the cover pieces, and needless to say, the lady didn't win—but she did enjoy the company."

"I bet she loved my little guys," Gram said. "Boys, would you like a treat?" She reached for a round metal box.

"Flower cookies! I love them," Alex said. Her grandmother gave a satisfied grin.

"Stick out your finger," Gram directed. Ty pulled his out of his mouth with a loud pop, and on it Alex hung a scallop-edged butter cookie with an open center. She did the same for Chandler.

"The flowers are blooming!" she declared.

They wiggled them and paraded around the room. Chandler stopped to look at his cookie and then at his other hand. He turned and held it out.

"One more right here," he said, sticking out a finger.

"You win," she said. "I knew it wouldn't take long to figure it out. Come on over, Ty. I have two more blossoms."

"It's wonderful to see how good you are with your brothers, honey," Grandma said to her. "It helps to have you all here. I really love the picture you drew for me, and the new TV is great."

"I'm glad," Alex said, feeling herself relax as she sank into a chair to listen to them chat about Gram's recuperation.

"Where are the boys?" her mom asked. She jumped, wide-eyed when she realized how quiet the room had grown.

"Don't worry," Gram said, "I know what you're thinking, but all of the medicines are in a pushcart. The nurses lock it up when they bring us our pills." They scrambled to look for the twins while Grandma leaned forward to watch the action from her bed.

They checked with the nurses, but Alex had another idea. She recalled seeing an empty name-tag holder beside an open door when they were coming down the hall. It was now almost closed. She nudged it wider and peered in to discover one of her little brothers on each bed, snuggled deep into a fluffy pillow and fast asleep. Without waking them, Alex went to find the others. The head nurse said they could stay there, but the safety rails had to be up.

Anne helped her mother settle into the wheelchair when the lunch trays arrived, and Alex asked Gramp to come with her on a tour. She especially wanted to see the therapy room.

There they found a gentleman walking between parallel bars. He clutched the rails and proceeded slowly with his instructor close by, murmuring encouragement. Alexandra felt the same pride of accomplishment she saw on his face when his goal was reached. He glanced up to discover his audience.

"That felt so good I think I'll do it again," he said.

They found another room that had exercise tables and floor mats, where legs and arms weakened by an operation, illness, or injury are worked.

The day after surgery, a young helper explained, Alexandra's grandma began her strengthening exercises here. Her limbs were moved to relieved the soreness and to begin the process of firming muscles and stretching tendons.

Most patients begin to put weight on their legs very quickly. They progress from the parallel bars and walkers to hopping, tiptoeing, and walking on mats that simulate uneven surfaces like sand, gravel, and grass. They lie on the mats and learn to get to a sitting position, then to stand.

The best encouragement for recovering patients, Alex learned, came with their first day-trip, visiting their own homes with the therapists going along to see what obstacles they might encounter and how they'd be able to manage them. Then follows two more weeks of practice to get ready for the happy move back home.

"The boys are on the loose again!" came Mom's plaintive cry. "They must have climbed down from the foot of the beds and wandered off." They soon found them seated quietly, watching the beautiful zebra finches flit about a glass aviary in a nearby hallway.

"Hectic morning?" Gramp asked, as he glanced over at his daughter-in-law.

"Whatever makes you say that? My mother's had a busy time, too. She'll soon have her therapy and a rest."

"She'll need a good massage after this visit!" Alex said.

"I'm so glad I came," Alex said at lunch. "It was good to see Grandma and find out she's really okay." She slurped the remainder of her milkshake. "I'd like to do it again."

"I'm proud of you. You made her feel so good," her mother said, patting Alex's knee. "You can come with me anytime you want. We'll leave the boys home," she hurried on. "Dad will have hours of fun on hunt-and-search missions." She gave a soft giggle as she glanced at her dozing angels.

"Whoops!" said Gramp said from the driver's seat. "It sounds as if I'll be involved."

"We're ready for you men to do a little baby sitting—a whole day of it!" a grown-up feeling Alex informed her long-suffering grandfather.

Practicing for a Blue

"Morning," Alexandra mumbled when she appeared in the kitchen doorway, still clad in rumpled pajamas and worn slippers. She patted each twin on the head as she shuffled past them to her place on the built-in bench.

"Where's Mom?" she asked.

"The boys and I decided to let her sleep in," her dad said. "She needed the extra rest. Besides, we're having a good time, and we cooked. So, daughter, when you snooze, you lose!"

"It smells good. What did you make, guys?" she asked.

"Bacon," Tyler replied, picking up a piece to dangle under his sister's nose.

"Scrambled eggs," Chan said, "and toast."

"Is Gramp in the barn?" she asked?

"Un-huh, he's feeding the horses for me this morning. Rob's visiting his parents for the day."

"That means Gramp will have to help Skylyn and me practice," she said, reaching to snitch a bacon strip from Ty's plate. This year for the first time they had permission to enter events in the Autumn Rodeo Festival. It meant a lot of hard work, and they were anxious to get started.

"I'll help later on. I talked to Joe and Aggie Eaglefeather yesterday, and they're bringing over Sky's horse. She'll do better with her own mount. By the way, Mom asked me to invite her to stay for the holiday weekend."

"That's great! Three days of fun!"

"Her whole family will be back Monday for our Fourth of July cookout too," he added.

"Maybe Sky's mom will make Indian frybread. I like it with honey; it's delicious," said Alex. "Thanks, Dad."

"Well, you deserve it. You've been a great help to your mother and me with all of our worries over Grandma. I really appreciate it."

"I wanted to," Alex said. "I love taking care of my brothers. It's more like fun than work." She bounced up to make a toast-and-jelly sandwich. She poured herself a cup of cocoa and dropped a few minimarshmallows on top to watch them bob around.

"Hot chocolate chases the early morning chill, but the cool air will feel good when Jess and I get going," she said.

"Everyone needs to work up a good sweat once in a while; it's great for the constitution!" he said with a chuckle as he popped the last bit of toast into his mouth.

"What?" she asked. "I thought we were celebrating the Declaration of Independence—don't mix me up, Dad!"

"It's an old fashioned saying, Al, that means exercise is good for a person's strength and well-being." Her dad was still laughing when Gramp walked in several minutes later.

"What's so funny?" he asked as he hung his hat and jacket on a hook.

"We're just having a little history lesson," her dad answered with a glimmer in his eyes.

"Boys, are they getting you prepared for college already?" He removed their empty plates and took them to the sink.

Alex walked past him and started toward the family room taking her cup of cocoa. Gramp followed and sat down in the recliner.

"Alexandra, I'm really proud of the way you took time for others yesterday. I don't think you realize how much joy you brought to those people just by talking to them. I watched you fix that lady's wheelchair. You helped her out in such a nice way. That's wonderful. My mother used to say, 'The smallest part of yourself given to others comes back threefold.'" Alex smiled her appreciation.

"I was surprised how easily they get around in wheelchairs. Even the people using walkers do just fine. And I couldn't believe how they visit with one another. They've turned themselves into one big family!"

"You're right. It's like an extended family. Most of them have similar problems, so they depend on each other for support. They even check on the ones confined to their beds."

"I'm thinking about asking if I could help with the bingo games. I could call out the numbers. B-6!" Alex demonstrated. "Doesn't that sound like fun?"

"Good idea. Some high school clubs encourage students to visit nursing facilities, and some kennels bring in their pets for visits. The patients love it. I'm sure the activities director would welcome some help. You sure are growing up to be a very nice young lady. I'm glad to be your grandfather."

"That's nice. Hey! Maybe we could take Chester and Goldie next time. They'd be a real hit."

"Oh, yes, right along with the twins. That would be double-double trouble. Don't even think of it!" he begged.

"I guess I'm good for your constitution!" she called back. She gave him a quick hug on the way out. He didn't see her wide grin.

"We need rain badly," Gramp said from his perch on a fence rail. "We're on a high-risk fire watch, kids. No fireworks for the Fourth this year. Just save them for another day."

"No sparklers, either?" Alex asked.

"Nope, nothing at all. Are we ready to work?" he asked as he jumped down. "I've sprinkled the corral so it doesn't become a dustbowl." He gave Alex and Sky a hand as they wrestled the saddles onto their horses.

Cowboys started having rodeos way back in the 1800s, but it was a long time before girls could compete. Rodeoing came out of pride in their work. They had steer-roping and riding contests with outfits they met along the trails during cattle drives. Men got together to do what they excelled in, and it was a good chance to see old friends and make new ones.

"Now are you slowpokes ready?" Gramp asked, pointing to his watch. "Get those hard hats on, and let's tackle the barrels!"

One of the most popular speed events, barrel racing is a contest in which a rider runs a cloverleaf pattern around a triangular course containing three barrels. The rider circles each barrel and after the third one makes a mad, seventy-five foot dash straight down the middle to the finish line.

"Lowest time wins; anything under eighteen seconds is a good score in that large arena," Gramp called. "Remember, I'm adding the regulation five-second penalty for each drum knocked over."

They started out executing slow circular patterns that eventually turned into figure eights. He finally introduced the barrels, and they walked repeat patterns around them. The dirt soon flew as they increased their speed. After a break, Gramp began timing their runs around the empty fifty-five gallon drums. They had a lot of laughs at their mistakes, especially when Alexandra signaled Jessie to keep to the right, but Jess, expecting her usual apple treat from Steven, made straight to the fence to greet him when he arrived.

"Alex, you have to keep control of your horse. You're in charge—show it!" Gramp instructed her. He removed his hat to shake off the dust and wipe his brow.

On a quick turn around a barrel, Skylyn slid from the saddle and ended up sitting in the middle of the corral.

"Lunch isn't being served out there!" Gramp hollered.

He began to line a wider path of stripes so they could ride side by side, simulating a race for the finish line.

"Ride low, lean forward!" Gramp yelled encouragement. "Put your hands on the horse's neck and run flat out for home just like a jockey!" Both girls were exhausted when the noon bell rang.

"Phew, the falls don't get any easier, and it's harder to beat the stopwatch. I got too many penalty seconds," Alex complained.

"Practice is the answer, and lots of it," her mom said.

"The biggest and best ribbon winners in bull riding get tossed off in the blink of an eye," Gramp reminded them as he sat down at the table. "They get right up and go to the next round."

"Think about it, Alex," her mom said, "your grandma's working the same way at learning to walk again."

"Thank goodness she doesn't have to ride a horse to get around. We'd have to put a motor on Jessie!" Alex said with a giggle they all joined in.

"I give up!" said Gramp raising his hands in surrender. "I've changed my mind; bring on the twins and the dogs—they're all saner!"

"Girls, you both did much better this afternoon, and you've got two months to sharpen your skills," Gramp said. "They'll have a keyhole race just for kicks again this year. Rob will be back tomorrow, and he'll work with you on that—he loves those flying finishes!"

"'Turning the key' is fun, and so is pole bending. We'll set up a course for you to thread your trusty steeds through," Alex's dad said, much to their delight.

Racing against the clock, contestants fly down a chalk-lined pathway, turn inside of the keyhole shape at the end, and race back. The best time wins. A rider is disqualified if his horse steps outside of the lines. In pole-bending events, a rider leaves the start, races past a line of six upright poles, rounds the farthest one, and begins weaving through them. He retraces the same pattern for a total of eleven turns. That done, he gallops to the start-finish line. Penalties occur for knockdowns.

"Skylyn, you're getting good on turns, nice and smooth, so the barrel's just the race for you. Alex, Jessie is very light-footed and agile, and she's great on long runs. She'll give you the fast finish needed for pole bending and keyhole. Know what, kids? I do believe you two have a good chance to bring home some color."

"You're talking blue ribbons, Dad?" she squeaked. He gave her a wink and two thumbs up. "Yes!" Alex yelled. She urged Jessie closer to Sky to smack high-five's and pumped her fist in the air.

"Sky, this is the first time in history that we'll be anxious for September to come!"

Book II

Skylyn

Coyote Ranch

Jangling bells and a chorus of bleats echoed in Joseph Eaglefeather's ear when his flock surged against the heavy wire fence. He greeted each by name as he unhooked the gate. Twenty-five scrubby churro sheep and nine angora goats spilled out and hurried up the lane toward the pasture.

Aware of the daily barnyard routine, the resident Plymouth Rock rooster gave a squawk and sidestepped the hoof of a frightened lamb searching for its mother.

"Rocky, my feathered friend, I'm glad you've learned to stay out of their way," Joseph told the black-and-white fowl.

Rocky fluffed out his feathers, shook his fiery red comb, and flew to the handle of an old wheelbarrow. Satisfied, the haughty bird folded his wings and made himself comfortable. He knew that when the noisy crowd dispersed, he and the hens could freely roam the corral and lean-to in search of tasty bugs stirred up by the trampling feet.

Comfortably watching from a deep window seat in the kitchen,

Sky was happy to have her dad on vacation and doing what he liked best. She laughed when Buff, the friskiest of her mother's hand-picked goats, sneaked up and butted Joseph as if urging him to grab his walking stick and come along. Settling back to enjoy the scene, she sipped her milk and caught a glimpse of their old English sheep-dog. Ever serious about his work, Shep sped ahead, circling his charges to keep them close and safe from harm.

Skylyn pulled her shiny black hair into a ponytail, securing it with a silver clip dotted with chunks of turquoise. Allowing her gaze to drift around the den, she admired the honey-colored Indian drums, now glass-topped that served as tables. Sky was proud of her father's collection of Native American artifacts accenting the freshly painted walls. She loved the turtle-shaped rattle made of rawhide adorned with horsehair and feathers dangling from small, tin-cone tinklers. But her favorite was a pony bow with its arrows nestled deep in a fringed quiver. Sunlight picked up the warm colors of her mother's woven goods scattered on the terra cotta tile. Early Navajo shepherds like her grandfather and her great-grandfather wandered the southwest desert for hundreds of years, following their unique breed of sheep from whose wool the women wove their blankets and rugs.

With a growing interest in art, Sky thought of the natural pigments nestled in her paintbox. Let's see, she mused, what great artist would use these shades of black, gray, apricot, cream, and that rare dark brown called—the treasure of the Navajo? "I think Georgia O'Keeffe would just love them," she whispered, answering her own question.

Spaniards brought the churro to America early in the 1500s. Valuable for the double coat of greaseless wool, they've been carefully guarded by Navajo shepherds for centuries. The lengthy fibers of its outer coat are coarse and strong. Handspun on wood spindles and wound into large balls of yarn, they are woven on vertical looms into items that became popular with early settlers and were offered for sale or trade. Recognized rug designs like Two Gray Hills, and early chiefs' blankets are highly prized by collectors today.

"Skylyn, I heard you laugh. What's so funny this early in the morning?" Aggie Eaglefeather asked.

"Ah, I was just making up a silly game—nothing great."

"How would you like to come to the gallery with your sister and me? Goodness knows, we have tons to do. I wish your brother were here to help uncrate boxes."

"Mom, did you forget I'm going with NanEagle to collect plant materials? And you know Taggart loves firefighting school," she reminded her.

Aggie gave her a big hug. "Have a great time, honey." She went to pour herself a mug of coffee, called for her elder daughter to hurry, and rushed out to her red Bronco.

Sky saw them off and made her way to the stable. She lovingly stroked her spotted appaloosa, Nambe, on his velvety nose before filling his feedbox with oats and the rack with hay. She did the same for the other equine occupants and stopped again at Nambe's stall to freshen his water.

"I'll be back later Nammie, and maybe we'll practice some extra runs," she promised. Sky and Alexandra were anxious for the upcoming rodeo and festival.

Wandering over to the little sod barn, Sky found Strudel, her toy poodle, lying beside the open door, chewing his left front paw.

"Hi pupski, what are you doing here? I thought you'd be off helping Dad and Shep. What's wrong with your foot?" She knelt down to check.

At first the little dog resisted her effort to inspect the paw by playing tug of war with it. He'd pull; she'd tug. He made a valiant attempt to escape but couldn't go far without limping badly, thus becoming an easy catch for Sky. Strudel gave in and let her examine it.

"No cuts," she said and looked farther. "Ah ha, I thought so! You've got a nasty thorn between your toes." Sky urged him to lie still. "Relax," she told him, "it's like getting a manicure—you'll love it afterwards." She talked softly as she worked out the sticker. "There, how's that?" He was too busy soothing the wound with his wet tongue to pay much attention. Eager to be off on her walk, Sky ran her hands through his curly coat and gave him a final hug.

"Phew! You need a bath!" she said, wrinkling her nose.

Strudel abruptly stopped licking, and his head snapped around. He scrambled up and took off at the speed of light. Zipping around the corner, he headed for the hills, leaving behind a trail of dust.

Skylyn laughed and jumped up to follow her canine friend. She spotted his bobbing pompom of a tail as he disappeared over a knoll on the sparse grazing lands, racing towards his pals, the Navajo sheep.

"It must have been that dreaded B-word!" she said to no one in particular.

"What bees are you talking about?" asked a voice at her elbow.

"Oh, NanEagle, you surprised me," Sky said, using her pet name for the woman who lived in the original part of their ranch house. Sky's late grandfather had constructed it himself from adobe bricks made with a mixture of red sandy clay, straw, and water. The old homestead now connected with a sprawling new addition. "I didn't know you were there. You walk so softly, just like the wind and the wild animals. I hope I can do that when I grow up. Bees? No, I was just talking to myself about Strudel needing a good bath. You can guess his answer."

"I do know how he feels about that. I saw your mother and sister leave for work. Are you ready to go with me?" she asked her youngest granddaughter. Sky nodded.

"Raven Lee's helping set up the new exhibit. Mom's excited about including her own weaving this time. Oh, did you hear? Dad found a basket for me," she said. "Come see. It looks a lot like the one on your back." She headed into the sod barn.

"An old and trusted friend," Nan said. Her face glowed with pleasure. "I had forgotten about it." She ran her hands around the smoke-darkened rim and saw Sky's puzzled look. "It's one of my old weavings," she added.

"You made this, Nan? When?"

"Many years ago, too long to remember," said the aged Indian woman. She stared beyond the barn's dark interior into the bright August morning, lost for a few moments in childhood memories. She motioned for Sky to turn around, lifted the dangling leather straps, and placed a rough, flat strip across Sky's forehead. "This padded piece is called a tumpline. It eases the load. The leather has hardened from years of being idle, but I will soften it for you," she said as she adjusted the basket on Sky's back. "My sisters and I were very young when our mother taught us how to prepare hides. We 'fleshed' elk, buffalo, and deer hides with bone or antler scrapers."

Skilled at tanning, Indian women began the process by stretching large skins out on the ground and pegging them, hair side down. They spent hours scraping away muscle, fat, and tissue. Using rocks and sticks, they worked in an oily mixture of animal brains and fat to soften the buckskin for clothing. It was then left to bleach in the sun. Winter garments retained the hair that was worn next to the body for extra warmth.

"Some of the older women chewed small strips of leather to make them supple," Nan recalled. They flattened and dyed porcupine quills and sewed them on along with colored beads. They decorated all kinds of clothing with their imaginative creations. It was good winter-time work."

"It's surprisingly light on my brow," Sky said, easing the rough band into place.

"When you have a load of sticks and grass weighing it down," Nan said, with a glint in her eye, "then we shall speak about comfort. For now, carry it on your shoulder."

Skylyn glanced up at the sound of chickens clucking softly to each other as they scratched about on the earthen roof.

"With this drought they'll find more dried seeds than fresh ones," Nan said. "But there should be a lot of things to collect for basket making."

"We'll just get Dad to do a rain dance; that'll solve it!"

Sod buildings, like the smaller of their two barns, were first constructed in the mid-1800s on the Great Plains, where timber was not readily available. Settlers cleared their newly claimed land and cut slabs of sod, which hardened to brick-like strength. They staked out a square and laid the thick slabs one row at a time, leaving space for a small window and a door as they built up the sides. The "soddie" roof was finished last. Long poles ran from front to back with shorter ones covering them from each side to the midpole. Layered with straw, brush, or grass, the whole roof was then covered with dirt and tamped down tightly. They hung hide or cloth over the openings until they could collect enough wood to make a permanent door.

"You know," Nan said, "if your dad dances too much, he'll have to pay the chickens to give the soddie a haircut!"

"I guess it'll be chickenfeed! Tag always complains that's all his weekly paycheck amounts to." Sky returned the tease, making both of them laugh.

The two started out toward the mountain. Just southwest of them Sky saw her father slowly urging the animals on to forage in the shadow of the distant hills.

"They'll be happy when they get to the woods. They love to browse on the shrubs," Sky said. She blew on the bone whistle her dad had made; he turned and waved his hat in response.

"We'll be more comfortable among the trees, too," Nan said. "Right now I'm thirsty." She pointed to a log nestled in a fringe

63

of brown-tipped ferns and made her way to it. "Let's stop and have a drink."

"That's the best idea yet, Nan." As Sky unfastened her canteen from her belt, two lemon-yellow butterflies shimmered by. The pair steered their rollicking flight toward the patches of cow clover and wild carrot struggling to grow despite the heat. Magically, in late summer the carrot would produce beautiful white flowers known as cow parsnip, or Queen Anne's lace. Reaching the size of saucers, the tall, frilly blooms play hostess to scores of ecstatic bumblebees.

"Tell me more about when you were young, Nan. I love your stories," she said.

"Well, I remember living in a small red-dirt, mound home called a hogan when I was little. I was born in it, far away from here near Navajo Mountain in Arizona. No one would go onto that sacred mountain, but we stayed close by to gather berries and dig vegetables.

"My dad was smart, and he was a good carpenter. I watched him make the heavy door and its thick wooden frame. As a final touch he opened a slit under the crossbeam to let smoke out and a little light in. We stayed warm and dry most of the time. Later on, he made us a larger, traditional Navajo adobe lodge."

Like sod houses, early fork-stick hogans were primitive dwellings suited to arid areas, and they were easy to construct. Sky had often been to the museum in town and seen the diorama showing step by step how one was made.

"Picture tepees were very special," Nan continued. "They were painted to show the brave deeds of the owners. Warriors drew tribal symbols and battle records on the outside, but the extra linings, stuffed with dried grass for insulation, had designs done by the women. I helped my mother; she made it into a game for us. She was a good painter and teacher."

Nan told Sky how the Amerinds, as American Indians are called, learned from their earliest ancestors how to make paints and dyes. Gathering certain seeds, leaves, pods, and roots, they ground them up with stones in cups hollowed out of flat rocks. Adding the powder to the water heated by red-hot stones made the colors come to life.

"I felt very grown up when I was allowed to prepare the dye. The berries gave up their colors so easily when we mashed them," NanEagle said with glistening eyes.

"I love to use your grinding stones to make corn meal," Sky said, "especially when you bake us cornbread with it."

"Those stones were my mother's. They will be yours when you have a family someday," Nan promised.

Silent for awhile, they both took a last sip of water. NanEagle slipped her bottle into its pouch and began to rise. She quickly sat back, touched Sky's arm, and put a finger to her lips.

"What?" Sky whispered. Nan shook her head, her eyes busy searching the wooded area. They heard a twig snap and froze.

"Look, there—cougar! Stay still."

In an uphill thicket, nose to the ground, a tawny cat sniffed at a large, leaf-covered pile. Intent on its task, it slowly pawed at the brush, sending out small showers of dirt and leaves. Stopping often to rest, it lay with its head on a front paw. The two visitors to this magnificent creature's domain stared in awe at the remarkable sight.

"It's found a food stockpile. We're downwind, so it doesn't smell us. This one's lucky to find something; they usually only eat at night, and they like fresh-killed game," Nan said.

"Dad will need to keep a close watch on the sheep," Skylyn whispered.

The puma kept working until it unearthed the carcass of a mule deer. It began to gnaw at a leg bone, happy to fill an empty stomach. Sky and her grandmother relished the rare view of such an elusive animal.

The mountain lion, largest of the American cats, ate its fill and left its larder to find water before seeking a cool place to sleep. It slowly limped away.

"There's the answer, granddaughter, an injury. It had to eat carrion or starve." Skylyn nodded.

"Strudel had a little foot problem this morning. I was there to fix it, but the cat has to figure out how to help itself."

"Long ago I saw a cougar image chipped in a stone by the ancient ones. The tail was curved across the top of its body, and it had long claws. My father and his people loved to travel in the summertime and camp way out on the plains. As we moved along he pointed out lots of images painted on cliff walls and in caves we'd explore. He said they helped the people remember the past. It is very old art," Nan said as she and Sky moved on through the forest.

"I know what you mean—stone carvings are called *petroglyphs*, and painted pictures that tell stories are *pictographs*. Mom has a lot of books about prehistoric art," Sky said, showing off a bit.

"You told me it was the women's job to take care of the tepees, Nan. Did they do it alone? I can't believe my mother would be able to!" Sky said, moving around miniature wild rose bushes, resisting the urge to pick a tiny pink bouquet to take home in her carrier. "There's no moving our big house now, that's for sure!" They both laughed at the idea.

"Women made tents. It took a long time, so they turned it into a party with the new owner providing the food." NanEagle paused to think. "They'd cut tall lodgepole pines and skin off the bark. The tepee's opening always faced east to greet the rising sun and the dawn of a new day. At night, the creaking of those lodge poles moving in the prairie wind was so comforting. I always felt so safe and secure.

"You're right, Sky, those women had to work awfully hard. It took a lot of bison hides to cover a tepee. Sewing them together couldn't have been easy—they used strips of animal ligaments threaded into antler or bone needles. But any Indian woman was able to put a tent up in fifteen minutes or less," Nan bragged.

"That quickly?"

"Yes, and striking it was even faster." She beamed, waving her hand. "Three minutes to get one down."

"Wow, I'd like to see that! It would make a neat contest, almost like in a rodeo," Sky said with a laugh. Nan seemed to know all there was about how Indians built their homes.

"Mother gave my sisters and me the job of pounding the wooden pegs through the bottom of the hides to steady our tepee against the wind. We'd also help collect heavy rocks to place around the edges. Stone tepee circles are still found in remote places on the plains," Nan said.

"I bet that's an awesome sight. I'd love to find one."

"My grandfather told me that when lookout scouts warned of approaching enemies, they simply mounted their horses and fled, abandoning the entire campsite."

"Oh my, I forgot about the Indian wars with the soldiers. They were sad."

"That's a story for another time," NanEagle promised.

They found the willow bushes Nan had been seeking. Their branches would serve as a basket's base and sides. She showed Sky how to remove the leaves and tie the stripped willow rods in bundles with pieces of long grass.

"When we get home, I'll put them in water to soak for about three days to make them soft and easy to bend. I'll start the basket by forming the end of a rod into a small loop and sewing it with the grass-weaver." Nan will continue to coil and sew until it forms a flat bottom. The sides will grow as she lays one rod on top of another, catching each stitch to the wrapped coil below. "Perhaps I'll weave in a design by including materials of different colors. Would you like to work along with me and make one of your own?" Sky had intended to watch everything her grandmother did, but the invitation was even better. If only they didn't have to wait those three days to get started.

Red-winged blackbirds gave their twisting "kink!" call in noisy chorus with resident frogs as the travelers neared the marshes. Beavers had once made an intricate canal system to transport logs to the pond, but now it was clogged with cattails begging to be harvested. Sky got busy cutting their leaves. Interrupted in its quest for dinner, something slithered right across her foot. "Yikes!" She yelped and scrambled out of the way. Remembering her dad's teaching, she recognized it as a common garter snake. The harmless green reptile took its yellow-striped body elsewhere to continue hunting minnows and tadpoles in peace.

"I was almost a snack for a snake," she reported.

"They have to eat, too," her grandma replied.

"I've seen birds carrying cattail fluff and thistle down to line their nests," Sky said after a while.

"Well, my dear girl, Indian babies had it stuffed in their cradleboards to keep them dry, just like today's diapers! It served them very well, too," NanEagle said.

"How smart! We learn from books, but they borrowed ideas from nature," Sky said.

"Now you're tuning in to the old earthly rhythms." Nan stood up to stretch. "It's a kind of easy, working harmony that benefits all who take time to care. Good for you, Granddaughter."

NanEagle stopped in a grove of firs to remove her basket and retrieve a package from it. She spread a cloth on a springy bed of pine needles and set out a late picnic lunch.

"We'll gather some yucca leaves in the valley on our way home. They make good weavers," Nan said, unwrapping their sandwiches.

"It's so peaceful here. What a nice way to spend the day. I love being outdoors," Sky said between sips of cold juice.

"Look over there!" She pointed at a chipmunk sentry perched on its haunches atop a boulder. It was munching on a fir twig that jiggled in its mouth. As it dined, the little rodent surveyed its home turf, which seemed to be in perfect order until Sky forgot herself and blurted out "It's got a mustache!"
The startled guardian of the clan issued a sharp chip! of warning and made a mad dash for its hole.

"Animals are so comical. I don't know what we'd do without them," Sky said.

"This land used to be filled with beaver," Nan told her. "Mountain men trapped them until there were almost none left. Long ago my family and I saw a trading hut covered with their brown pelts along with those of wolf, fox, mink, ermine, and bear. More were stacked in huge piles to be shipped east. The owner said city folk would have coats and hats made of them. Looking at the traps made me sick. Sometimes our people accidentally got caught in the hidden metal jaws. Awful as it was, they could pry them open, but trapped animals were left to suffer, sometimes for days, before dying a horrid death," Nan said with a shiver.

"My mom told us about what happened to her tabby cat," Sky began. "It got caught in a trap a neighbor set in the woods behind his house. The cat couldn't get free and was gone for two days. It chewed off its own foot and limped home holding up what was left of its forepaw. Mom said she cried so hard for the poor thing. Her grandfather dressed the wound and stitched a leather pouch with a drawstring to cover it. She said she never loved him as much as she did right then. Thank goodness the cat got well. It learned to walk on three legs and lived out the rest of its eight lives."

"Bless you, dear Skylyn, for telling me. I will cherish it always. Animals, whether it's your poodle or our beautiful cougar friend today, have a strong will to survive and to withstand whatever people do to them."

"Dad says Indians took only what they needed to live on so the animals and plants wouldn't die out," Sky reminded her. "He called it 'preserving the ecology.' We all have to work hard to save our land and its wildlife."

"Let's hope it's not too late," NanEagle added quietly.

Traveling home through ponderosa pine and juniper along a trail once used by trappers, they slowly left the rolling hills for the low desert behind the ranch. A lone coyote scanned the baked arroyo floor from which water had been absent for months. Pinyon pine, spruce, and sagebrush tried to survive on its rim next to the yucca Nan was looking for. She cut a few of its flat underleaves as Skylyn studied the beautiful yellow blooms that grew on spikes.

Most were now going to seed, their pods bronzed by the sun.

"My basket's getting heavy!" Sky complained as she shifted the pack to her back. "How did Indian women carry all the stuff they needed? I bet they had to gather firewood, as well, so they had to be strong. It must have been hard to care for their families."

"Now you have an idea of what it took for people to survive," Nan said. "And, my dear, you've also learned why this kind of carrier is known as a burden basket."

Back home, Sky helped her grandmother spread everything they'd collected on the ground near the soddie to dry. NanEagle went off for a nap. Sky went in to wash her hands and have a cold soda. She finished her regular chores and headed to the corral to set up some bright-blue steel drums for barrel-racing practice.

Nambe was happy to walk the cloverleaf course around the barrels at first. Sky soon increased their speed, racing for a faster finish.

"We're getting better, boy," she said. "No knock-downs, no penalties today! Hooray!"

Nambe had earned his reward, a cool bath in the new shower stall attached to the stable. The two long ropes hooked to each side of his halter bobbed as he danced under Sky's splashes and squirts.

"Nammie, settle down. I know you love it, and I have to be quick to save water," she said to the frisky horse. Three of the boarding horses, clustered in the shade of a spreading tree, hung their heads over the corral rails and watched in envy.

"I'll get to you as soon as I can," Sky assured them.

Nambe's ears twitched when she began to brush his mane. "What do you hear?" Sky asked, pausing to listen. "Ah, I bet the sheep are coming; you always pick up their bells before I do."

The dusty herd went directly to their enclosure to rest. Joseph waved a greeting as he strolled over to latch the gate.

"Hi, Dad." Sky moved up to lean on the fence.

"There's nothing like the mountains in the heat of summer," he said with a vigorous nod that wobbled his wide-brimmed straw hat. "Did you have fun reaping the harvest of the hills, honey? I used to go with Ma a long time ago, and I loved it."

"It was great. I'll go with her anytime. Dad, there's an injured cougar up there. We think it's fairly young." Sky went on to explain.

"Thanks for the warning! I'll keep my eyes open for it. John needs to be aware of it when he takes the sheep out next week," he said.

"Where's Strudel?" she asked.

"Strude was with us all day. He's probably still with Shep," he said, starting toward the house.

"No, I saw Shep lying in the barn." Where is that little bugger? she wondered. Starting off to check the stable, she circled it twice and whistled. On a slow jog past the sheep pen, she thought she caught a glimpse of him. Climbing the heavy wooden gate, she counted five cream lambs relaxing with their mothers in the shaded crib. The rest of the flock stood in front of the hut, sharing a cud-chewing session with the shaggy mohair goats.

Where could he be?

"Wait a minute—we only have four lambs! Strudel, you big baby, come out of there! You know exactly why I want you, and you're hiding!" Sky hitched both legs over the gate and jumped into the pen just in time to see Strudel crawl under a large nanny.

"Don't you protect him, Dorothy! He's mine!" she declared. Dorothy soon had good reason to shift her hindquarters when Sky slowly applied her full body weight against them. No sign of him.   "Wouldn't you think these mothers would understand a kid needing a bath at the end of a busy day. But, no-o-o, not this woolbearing bunch of walking horseblankets!" Sky groused at them.

"Okay, you rugrats, who has him? He can't get out, so he must be in," she reasoned. No answering bleats, no tinkling bells.

"All right! I'll deal on your level. Can't beat 'em?

Join 'em!" she announced. Dropping to her hands and knees she crawled around the stubborn, hoofed convention to no avail; they stuck together as if one.

Creeping close to Buff, the beige billy goat, she saw Strudel dash for a different breed of cover.

"Little dog, you think you're related to these animals just because you have curly hair!" she spat out, trying hard to wedge her shoulders between twin rams who were determined to have no part of her sport.

"We'll cure that with a poodle cut to match your silly tail!" she huffed, peering under yet another bearded chin.

"Wolf!" she yelled. That would surely do it. She rose to her knees... "Nope, I guess you don't know that story. Maybe..." She stood and cupped her grimy hands around her mouth. "Chow time!" Sky held her breath and waited.

She glanced at another woolly critter just as the off-white poodle ran to snatch a quick peek at his food dish. Skylyn executed a perfect dive.

"Gotcha, you little sneak!" she cried, scuffling with the wriggling dog. She held him high and glared at the flock.

"And you guys," she vowed, "just wait until next spring when I get hold of the shears!" She stuck her nose into the air, turned on her heel, and stalked off to the sound of rousing applause.

"Well, Strudel, I see that we have two more black sheep in the family," Sky's mom said as she reached over the fence to pat him and her surprised daughter on the head.

"Yep," her dad said. Taking the last sip from his can of iced tea, he thumped it down on a post. "But I can fix that. C'mon, I'll meet you at the horse shower!"

"Naw, Dad, forget that," Raven said with a wide grin and a perfectly mimicked bleat. "I'd just send them both out to the nearest dry cleaners!"

Rodeo

"Welcome, folks! Glad y'all could make it to our annual Fall Rodeo Festival right here in beautiful Indian Steps, Colorado." The music slowly rose over the announcer's invitation to give a hearty hand to the guys and gals in the parade!

Clods flew from silver horseshoes when a double row of riders carrying poles sporting colorful flags and long streamers raced to the middle of the oval arena. Separating to dash past each grandstand, they crisscrossed midway and formed a large circle. A pair of trumpets heralded a cowboy astride a white stallion. Emotions ran high when the wind, working its magic, unfurled the Stars and Stripes as he sped around the ring. He wheeled into the center and pulled to a halt. Everyone rose and remained standing for the national anthem.

Skylyn's parents, sister, and grandmother sat in the middle of the fourth row with the Tanners, seated just behind them.

"Oh, I hope our surprise for Alexandra gets here on time," Anne Tanner said, settling Alex's twin brothers beside her.

"And that the girls get to see some of the opening festivities."

"I bet they're quaking in their best boots and buckskins back in the waiting area!" Sky's dad said reclaiming his seat.

"Probably, but they'll be fine. By the way, Steven," Aggie asked Alex's dad. "Did Rob register for any of the events? He's great at roping and bronc busting."

"Our pal, Wrangler Rob, signed up early this morning," Steven said. He leaned forward to include his wife. "Rob called Gramp on the car phone. He's left the airport and should be here shortly. Well, boys," he checked his program. "I think you'll enjoy the next act, then the barrels begin. Sky's up third, and Alex drew the last ride."

Native Americans in beautiful feathered costumes entered, accompanied by the deep vibration of hide drums. The crowd watched spellbound as a young man skillfully performed an intricate hoop dance to their pulsing rhythm. At the end awed silence turned into tumultuous applause.

Fun became the order of the day when stubborn, long-eared mules ridden by clowns in fright wigs appeared. The animals balked at any attempt to stay on them for more than a few moments, pitching off their ridiculous riders in a whirl of flying arms and legs.

With encouragement from their parents, youngsters in the crowd were invited to enter the boot race. A clown with a large top hat and red rubber nose rolled out balanced on a barrel, feet working fast to propel it along. Hopping off, he directed them to remove their footwear and place it neatly on a line drawn across the dirt. He escorted them back to the starting line, keeping everyone laughing with silly jokes and his best tumbling tricks. They never saw the two zany characters sneak out of a holding chute behind them and paid no attention to the chorus of catcalls that arose from the audience.

Working fast, the newcomers scrambled the boots and piled them high.

At the command of "On your mark!" and to the shouted advice

from the grandstand, the contestants turned to discover the wobbly tower of leather. The first one to retrieve his boots, slip them on, and dash back to the finish won. The prize? A pony ride around the arena led by a clumsy fellow in gigantic black patent shoes.

"Riders up!" Alexandra's grandfather called.

"It's time? Goodness, I don't think I'm ready yet," Sky said, fidgeting with her hat and new shirt. But she grabbed Nambe's reins and mounted.

"Me either," Alex said, resting her forehead against her horse's shoulder. She rechecked her stirrups and wiped her palms on her jeans.

"Come on now," he said, "you've been training months for this day." Alex slowly pulled herself up into the saddle. The girls were grateful to Gramp Tanner as well as their fathers and Rob Stanley for their patient instruction at practice.

"All right," Alex muttered to Jessie. "Let's go." She leaned forward in her saddle; nothing happened.

"Al," Gramp said with a laugh. "You've got to do better than that."

Sky tugged at her safety hat, patted her horse one last time, and started off, beckoning her friend to follow. She disappeared around a corner, but Alex stayed put.

"Are you sure we can do it, Gramp?" she whispered. "Our rivals look much bigger than I imagined." He pulled at his Stetson and moved closer.

"Those girls are in your age group," he said for her ears only. He pried her hand from the reins and rubbed it. "You know, honey, the first step in any journey is the hardest one to take." He looked deep into her eyes. "You don't have to do this if you don't want to. "You can try again next year. It's up to you..."

"Alex, guess who I just saw in the stands?" Skylyn reappeared, sitting tall on Nambe.

"I can't; you tell me."

"Your grandmother is here! She's right in back of NanEagle and Raven. I saw her come in with Rob."

"What? She flew out here for the rodeo? I can't believe it!" she cried. With a smile climbing her face she turned Jess toward the arena. "Let's go to the fence guys. I want to wave to her before I start."

"We're right behind you!" Gramp answered for them both, and Sky grinned at him.

"I guess that did it, huh, Mr. T.?"

He wiped his brow on his sleeve. "Phew!" he whistled and motioned her on. "That cinched it, Sky."

"Please, don't say that word," she groaned. "I must have checked Nammie's rigging a zillion times already!"

"Okay," Gramp said. "You know the drill: just connect the big green dots. You're set for a day of fun. Go get`em, cowgirl!"

"Up next: Skylyn Eaglefeather from Coyote Ranch in Mesquite. Time to beat is eighteen point two seconds," the announcer advised. The klaxon had barely died away when they heard him exclaim, "Whoa! Look at that one go!"

Nambe burst through the gate at a furious pace, crossed the starting mark, and angled right, holding steady to the first barrel in the cloverleaf pattern. Sky sat deep in the saddle to help him make a tight right turn. Part way round an inner alarm sounded. No-o! Did I brush the drum? She glanced back, saw it wobble and slowly settle itself. Relieved, she pressed on to attack the second. They cleared it clean! "Good boy, Nammie!" she cried, rushing on to take the last can.

No penalty points, her mental dialogue continued...roll back at half barrel then sprint...

They approached number three, barrel-side left. Sky pulled out slightly wide, more than they'd practiced! Nambe stumbled; his ears flickered. "It's okay, boy, don't worry!" He regained his footing, neatly pivoted at the turn, and plunged straight ahead, sprinting the seventy-five feet to the finish line.

On their feet for the whole time, both families had been tracing every step of Sky's ride, cherishing her first go at competition. Sky pulled Nambe up to a skidding halt and checked the board when the announcer exclaimed,

"17.3 seconds! That'll be hard to beat," he added.

Six more young entries worked their mounts through the course, all within the eighteen second time range. Perched on a fence rail, Skylyn held her breath as each score flashed up.

"You're next, Al," Gramp warned. He saw her lips form a tight line, her eyes narrow. He swallowed hard. What on earth is she thinking?

"I'm going to start slightly back of the gateway, Gramp. It'll give us more speed." He nodded.

"Your choice," his low voice rumbled. "Take a deep breath and just do it."

Alex pried her gaze from his, spoke quietly to Jessie, and moved to the end of the alley. She signaled "ready" to the starter, heard the buzzer and her grandfather's call: "Hustle!"

She gave Jess her cue, pressed the reins down on the horse's neck, and leaned forward. Racing through the entrance, they bolted into the arena and passed the white line to activate the clock.

In the stands Anne gasped and grabbed her husband's hand. She knew Alexandra was in for the ride of her life!

Jessie charged dead ahead, dug her heels into the loose dirt, and swung right to circle the first steel drum. Alex issued a booted nudge to Jess's flank and pointed her in the direction of the next dark green obstacle. There the horse angled her pattern left. Alex sat back in the saddle to help execute a deep, rolling turn. She tightened her leg against Jess's tummy and toed in sharply. Easily clearing the barrel, they drove forward. "One more, girl," she encouraged.

"Stay calm; we'll slow before this next one," she reminded Jessie as they rushed toward the drum at the top of the cloverleaf. She shifted both reins to one hand and gripped the pommel with the other. They wheeled to the right "Now!" she cried. Jess swiftly gathered her forward motion and focused her beautiful liquid eyes on the long raceway home.

Alex imagined Gramp's familiar voice saying,

"Ride low, lean forward, just do it." And so they did. They blazed a hot trail, arrow straight, to the finish.

"Bring it on in!" Gramp hollered through cupped hands as he stood tall on his seat at the bottom of the stands. He looked down as they flew by, Jess's tail sailing straight out. Alex pulled leather and whipped around in the saddle to check the leader board.

"Holy cow, seventeen seconds flat!! You did it!" he shouted. The scoreboard agreed. The crowd roared when the announcer declared Alexandra, riding Jessie, the winner. She tore off her hat and waved it to her ecstatic family. Generously patting and praising her horse, she set out in search of her best friend.

Jessie's body heat mingled with Alexandra's. She fanned herself with her gloves and longed for a drink of water, all the while thanking her many well-wishers.

"Have you seen Sky?" she asked several along the way.
No one had.

Gramp came around the grandstand wall shouting.

"You and Jess! Just plain raw horse power in action!"
She bent for a hug, only to have him haul her from the saddle and swing her in a big circle. The others came, fighting their way through the crowd to get to her.

"Gramp, do you know where Sky is?"

"She ran into the stands to watch you cross the finish. She'll be here."

"She got second place, didn't she?" Alex twisted the handkerchief he had given her. "Is she happy about it?"

"Loves it! Says she'll catch up to you on the next round!" He saw her face clear of worry.

"Thanks, Gramp. We couldn't have done it without you. You're the best!"

"You did it, missie, not me. It's your blue ribbon. You worked hard for it, so savor the triumph."

"There isn't the slightest chance of forgetting my first rodeo win," she said.

"Alex!" came a shout. "We're one-two!"

Skylyn launched herself at Alexandra and wrapped both arms around her surprised friend. They rocked back and forth with Sky still chanting, "First and second! Wow! You really flew!"

"You did, too—I saw your run!"

"It was okay," Sky shrugged. "I made a couple of mistakes."

"Small ones. Be glad you didn't get any penalties. Next time you'll do great," Alex encouraged.

"I hope so! You want help putting Jessie in her stall? Then we can go get something to eat before our afternoon events."

Their parents made a quick visit to congratulate the girls. Alex's grandma declared them the best rodeo riders she'd ever seen.

"Gram," Alex teased, "that's just because you've never been to one before."

"I have," NanEagle spoke up, "and I think you're not only good competitors, but also the best of friends. I'm proud of you."

After giving Sky and Alex permission to visit the livestock exhibits, the two families left to see the women's barrel racing.

"We'll be back for our pole-bending event and to watch Rob compete," the girls promised. They were anxious to see the Indian tepees and the tomahawk toss.

"Whooosh! Thunk!

They felt the air move and stared openmouthed as the steel hawk slammed square into the center of a crude wooden target. Once a stout tree trunk, the stump now sat on a tripod surrounded by thick hay bales.

Alex and Skylyn walked with the thrower to retrieve the tomahawk. The wood squeaked as he pulled it loose, and he let them trace their fingers in the deep gash it left.

"Please do it again!"

"One more time," agreed their new friend, continuing to amaze them with his skill.

In honey-colored deerskin adorned with long fringes and touches of fur, the tall mountain man looked every inch a pioneer, complete with coonskin cap.

"It would have been just a game," he explained. "Neither trappers nor Indians threw their tomahawk very often. Unless they faced immediate danger, they wouldn't toss away a good tool. It never left a man's side, and was used for cutting firewood, as a hammer, and to skin furs. It was very necessary for survival."

"How did they get metal hatchets?" A boy inquired, taking his turn to touch the gleaming brass-tack patterns, a decoration favored by Indians, that accented the wood handle.

"The Spaniards brought them when their explorations began in the early fifteenth century. Amerinds were quick to recognize their value and were eager to barter for them."

"I think it was easier to do that than to spend hours making one," Skylyn said. The trapper agreed. He motioned them to sit on the split-log benches he had fashioned and placed near a small fire burning in a deep rock pit.

"Good thinking, young lady," he said. "But it took many years to accumulate enough European hatchets to supply everyone. Stone weapons continued in use for a very long time."

He went on to tell them about the knapping sites the ancients set aside to make their weapons. "Archeologists have discovered areas littered with chippings of flint or stone in caves, at gravesites, and under rock shelters."

"Some Pacific Northwest Indians carved ivory and whalebone into fishhooks and harpoons," the young man added. "They also used wood, horn, and antler," the trapper said. "Not many of those survived; they break down after hundreds of years in the ground."

He showed them his collection of stone projectiles and the metal points Amerinds had traded for. He picked up an arrow made from a stick. The notched base of the head was inserted in a split at one end then tightly wrapped with animal tendons called sinew.

"Cut feathers were *fletched*—attached to the opposite end—

and helped it fly true," he said. "They made spears the same way except for using longer sticks and larger points. Animal fat smoothed on the wrappings tightened as it dried and formed a strong bond." By now, several more youngsters had gathered round and were listening intently. He couldn't pass up the chance to talk about the ancient weapons he loved.

"About fourteen thousand years ago, very early paleo hunters used much longer lance points to kill the now-extinct woolly mammoths and saber-tooth tigers that roamed the land. It took a lot of spears to bring down such large prey. Many stone points have been found in mammoth-bone remains. Scientists were real happy with that discovery," he added, "because it proved that early man hunted those gigantic creatures."

"What were the littlest points used for?" Alex asked.

"Very small animals and birds," he replied. "Sometimes they carved the thicker end of an arrow shaft into a rounded shape called a bunt that merely stunned them."

"That's terrible!"

"Don't forget," he reminder her, "they worked hard and had to walk many miles to find food for their families." Still not satisfied, Alexandra wrinkled her nose at the thought.

"They chipped or "knapped" points using the thick end of a deer antler as a tool. A worker placed a stone on a heavy piece of hide resting on his knee and pressed the antler down along its edges and its face. He kept knocking off small fragments until he got the shape he wanted. He then chipped stems where the arrowhead attaches to the stick."

The trapper finished by showing them different sizes of T-shaped stone pieces with pointed tips.

"Anyone have any ideas how these were used?" No one could guess.

"They're drills—small ones for making tiny holes, and..."

"Larger ones for bigger holes!" his young audience finished for him.

"We have about twenty minutes before Rob's event," Alex

reminded Sky. They bought refreshments and hurried to the next exhibit.

Two elegant, painted tepees graced the fairground's landscape with their striking Native American artwork and vivid colors. Recapturing the spirit of the old West, one featured a galloping herd of wild mustangs. A dark brown buffalo with curved horns roamed the bottom half of the other. Its path was lighted by a full moon and yellow stars in the azure heavens above. Guarding the rear of the tepee, a warrior's rawhide shield hung on a stand made of sticks.

Going around to the front, the girls stepped into a warm, circular world recalling ages long past.

Alex counted sixteen cream-colored lodgepoles that bore the burden of supporting the huge bison-hide coverings. Two extralong poles held its smoke-wing flaps, now folded back at the entrance. Moving into the center, she looked up through a triangular maze of crossed poles to see the open smoke hole above. From the one nearest the door hung a leather bow case, and its matching quiver brimming with arrows.

A throbbing beat echoed in Sky's mind when she spotted a large powwow drum on the floor. It had cut elk antler for legs, and its side lacings held a pair of round-headed beaters in place. Her hands itched to try it.

"That's a beauty," she said. "Ours are covered with knick-knacks!" She vowed to do something about that when she got home.

An inner lining rose halfway up the tepee's sides. Tied to each wooden pole, it was gaily decorated with geometric designs. Alexandra peeked between the two layers.

"Look in here; straw stuffing for extra warmth in winter." Sky came to inhale the pure scent of sweetgrass.

"NanEagle said it kept raindrops from sliding down the frame," Sky told her.

When Skylyn saw Alex was busy exploring the back of the dwelling, she sat down cross-legged on the low platform that served as a bed and nestled deep in the bear-skin coverings.

"I always wanted to do this!" she confided to her partner.

"Isn't it comfortable?" a soft voice asked. Sky jumped up with a start.

"Oops! Sorry!" Sky apologized.

"Don't worry; everything's here for you to discover and learn." She pointed out two willow backrests accented with beads and feathers.

"I could use one of those when I do my homework," Sky declared, relaxing with a sigh. She sat down letting her weight anchor the bottom section, and leaned back with her legs stretched out. Thin rods tightly bound together with sinew down the center and sides formed the rest. Their hostess had placed its tripod in the ground behind to steady the top. Bright red cloth covered the end rods, adding a note of color and a touch of padding.

"I wish we could stay here all day," Alex said, looking around. Caught up in the soft golden glow, the two sat quietly surveying the ageless artifacts and absorbing the smell of worn leather. Reluctant to leave such peaceful surroundings, they paused to thank their guide. Popping out into the brilliant sunshine, they hurried toward the arena.

"I don't want to miss Rob's ride," Alex said, her boots clattering on the steps.

"And neither do the rest of his fans!" Sky added, following close on her heels as they scrambled into the seats Gramp had saved.

Rob waited with his arm resting on the pommel and his hat tilted forward studying the competition. His muscles tensed at each ride's end.

"Seems like 16:1 is the story of the day," he murmured.

Lincoln Jesperson, a friend from high school days, pulled in and checked the boards. Linc was happy to have the lead if only for a minute; he knew of Rob's ability on a horse.

"You're it, Robbie." Gramp leaned over the rail to warn his former student.

Rob urged Thunder, his sleek thoroughbred, a few steps back and paused with his attention riveted on the starter for the sign.

It came.

He applied boot pressure and Thunder ripped down the startway, entered to the delight of the die-hard rodeo fans, and tore up the dirt.

"Let's clean their clocks," boy!" Rob urged, heading for clover one.

He allowed the horse to do its job. Each can was a challenge, each simply met. "Head for home!" the young cowboy merely suggested as they swirled dust passing 'ole number three. Their tally now met, his mount complied.

Then, Rob had waited for it, depended on it, and sure enough it happened:

"Let Thunder roll!" his fans sang out.

Horse and rider raced across the chalkline to the chant and took a blue ribbon for their efforts.

"Like water off a duck's back!" Gramp yelled.

Rob just grinned and waved his hat to the delighted spectators; they clamored for more. He spoke to Thunder, who bent his right knee and dipped his head. Rob rode away amid the cheering.

"Fifteen point four!" Sky and Alex said shaking their heads. "How does he do it?"

"Better than that, how did Thunder learn to bow!" Alex asked.

"Practice! Practice! Practice!" Gramp couldn't help replying.

"So that's what he's been doing in the old corral." Alex snapped her fingers. "He said it was a secret he wouldn't share with any-one. I forgot all about it."

"Do you think ours could learn..." Sky began.

"I don't know," Alex replied, "but we can always try."

Oh, dear, what are they dreaming up now? Gramp could only wonder.

Nambe and Jessie, fresh from a good rest, shook their heads and flicked their tails. Up last to bend poles, Sky hung back from the start to give Alex room.

Jess danced sideways as Alex walked her in slow circles waiting for a rider to complete her run. She mentally traced the course of the six poles set twenty feet apart. Okay, two full strides between each one, she noted. The obstacles were embedded in rubber bases for safety, but she was glad she'd also wrapped Jess's legs. She leaned sideways to check them while Jess fidgeted.

"Whoa, girl. I know you're ready to run, and we're next." The knot in her stomach tightened when her number was called. Breathing deeply, she moved her restless horse into place.

Alex nodded to the starter. With a burst of stored-up energy Jessie streaked down the ramp, shot into the arena and flew pass the line of poles. Turning, she zigzagged between the six uprights. "Good so far, girl!" They had circled the last striped pole and turned to reweave the pattern when Jess's inner heel nicked its base. It teetered and fell. Penalty! her mind shouted.

"Keep going!" she urged Jess. One stride, change leads at pole two, turn, her legs cued Jess. Rounding clear they raced on. Three...four...five. Only the farthest pole remained. Jess's hindquarters slewed around it. Fired up and at full thrust, she aimed for the finish 105 feet away!

"Twenty point one seconds!" the announcer cried. "Including a five-second knock-down forfeit. Good ride!" Remembering her earlier showing, the crowd cheered. She headed back to find Gramp and catch Sky's ride soon to come.

"Nice finish!" Gramp congratulated.

"Points, though. Jess caught the pole," she said.

"Not to worry, honey. You were fast. It was a solid ride and great experience for everyone involved. You and your horse are real competition for the others, and that's good."

With a few last words to Skylyn, Gramp stepped back and watched her signal the starter. Nambe's power unleashed, he snapped out of the runway and zipped over the start line. They moved as one, swaying into each change of direction around the uprights. Trusting him, she let Nammie run his own race. Flowing smoothly, he navigated the course without fault. And now, the last pole...

"Go!" she shouted. Wind screaming past her ears, they flew straight to the line. No penalties. No problems. The noise level told her they'd given the spectators their money's worth. Wheeling Nammie, she got her first glimpse of the flashing board.

"Eighteen seconds flat!" Her shimmering eyes searched for her coach and found him holding two thumbs up!

"Dyn-o-mite!" Gramp yelled.

Almost in tears, she whipped off her hat and swung it at the crowd. Still in shock, she remained staring at the maze of blinking totals. "Gee whiz, Nammie, can it be?" she asked, stroking him, needing to talk.

Her thick plait of coal-black hair lay along her back as she moved out of the arena, head lowered, to brush away the tears on her cheeks. Gramp and Alex met her at the exit. He reached up, and she slid into his arms for a big hug.

"Honey," he said, clearing his throat, "you pushed your boundaries right out of sight!"

"You were awesome!" Alex told her. Sky hiccupped twice while they waited quietly, understanding.

"Alex came in third," Gramp said.

"That's great!" Sky said in between sniffles.

"What a day!" he massaged his neck. "I'm sure glad you two aren't into bull riding. I'd really be a wreck!"

"Please, give us a little time, Gramp. We've just started our rodeo careers!" He just groaned.

Pink cotton candy stuck to the tip of Skylyn's nose. It went unnoticed as she and Alex watched the bull riding event. The rider enters the ring from a chute. One gloved hand clutches a heavy rope wound around the bull's body just behind its fore legs, the other must remain in the air. Points are earned when the bull does lots of twisting and bucking, spurred on by the cowboy during an eight second ride.

"Kurt Raymond from Texas, up on Blue, outta chute seven!" the announcer intoned.

Left arm flailing, Kurt held tight. The angry bull whipped its back legs high and bucked hard, starting Kurt on a sideways slide. A fierce kick to the left set the number on to his shirt flapping as if it had grown wings; the next pitched him off.

He hit the dirt, executed a perfect roll, and popped to his feet. The clowns, good at their cowboy-saver jobs, distracted the animal while Kurt ran for the fence and clawed his way to safety.

No score. Total ride time, six seconds, with the crowd's appreciation his only reward.

"Rob's friend is up next on Killer," Alex said, worrying her lip. "That's a mean sounding name."

With a clatter of sharp hoofs, the snorting Killer emerged, head up, horns very much in evidence. Legs forward, Linc spurred hard, and they whirled to the right. The bull flipped its hind legs high, flinging Linc flat on its back. Just eight, he kept repeating to himself. Hang on for eight! The monstrous animal writhed, rocked, and twisted, but he stuck fast, praying for the buzzer. The instant it sounded he vaulted off and hit the ground running with his chaps dancing around his legs. The leader board blinked the score. "Eighty-three—a super ride!" proclaimed the loudspeaker. Killer, still loose and ready for revenge, charged a red-coated clown, who made a running dive into a protective barrel. Pointed horns knocked it over, and prodded it out of the way, delighting all. The bull snorted, scraped dirt, and went after a clown who lured him through an open gateway. The barrier banged shut.

Bam! Boom! Crack! Buddie is now in residence! The wooden pen vibrated under his thudding kicks. Rob grunted as he worked his heavy leather glove under the braided rope. Sweat glistened on his face and soaked his collar. Two men leaned in to help while a third waited ringside to set them loose.

"Unnnnaaah!" the gray Brahma bawled, clearly displaying his unhappiness.

"Whoa!" they coaxed.

Wrapping the end around his glove, Rob wriggled his way up and over the rope with his spurs forward.

"Ready?" the gateman asked.

Callused hands answered his nod, and the gate swung wide.

Buddie launched himself out of the pen with Rob staying firm as the animal bucked and looped, trying to shed the nuisance on his back. Rob's heels egged him on for extra points. "Pure brute power!" the announcer yelled from the press box above the stands when Buddie, arched high in spite of his massive bulk, picked that precise moment to snap a swift kick to nowhere in particular.

Rob was sure he knew where: We're in orbit! his brain reasoned, but "Ooo-ff!" was the sound he uttered. With Rob hanging on for dear life, man and beast reentered the Earth's atmosphere. Buddie's clanging bell announced their arrival. Please! his mind begged, how long can this last? The buzzer heard his plea and the clownmen rushed to his side. With plenty of power left over, Buddie jettisoned his rider. Rob's feet, hands, and bottom met the ground simultaneously. The jolt sent a stream of multicolored stars swirling before his eyes. He picked himself up and cased the area for good old Buddie before swaggering over to the fence.

All two thousand pounds of the bull, never unaware of the ex-rider, located their mark. Passing close to the fence on his path to the return pen, Buddie applied a swift brushback to the bottom of the cowboy's boots. Rob dived over, emerging red-faced, with a dent in his precious black Stetson, and a hint of a grin. The bull looked back only once, it seemed to everyone present, just to be sure.

"Ninety-five! Head for the winner's circle!" the speaker blared over the din.

"We're off to the Four-H exhibits," the girls reminded their parents, "and to check out that carnival on the next lot," they added.

"Stay together and be back by five o'clock. We're barbecuing," Sky's mother said. The two families had parked their RV's next to each other in the fair's campground.

Alexandra soon finished a red candy apple on a stick, and urged Sky to hurry and eat up.

"Soo-eee! It's swine city in here!" Sky exclaimed. "Oh, look at the adorable little piggies!" She leaned into a clean, straw-lined pen, delighted when the runt of the litter rustled through its bedding to sniff her hand.

"I love its curly tail! I want one!" Skylyn wailed when it found a finger and began to suckle it.

"Okay," Alex said. "Just put it with the sheep and goats, and Dorothy can baby-sit."

"She'd probably love it."

"You may pick it up," said a young girl, wearing a tag that said "Diana." "They're used to people."

Sky lifted the piglet out to cradle it in her arms. Rubbing its back produced a squeal of pleasure. Alex chose one to lavish attention on.

"Is this whole litter your entry?" Sky asked.

"Yes. They're Yorkshires. The mom was last year's winner. Come and meet her." She invited them to a nearby pen. They found a well-groomed, grand-champion sow with her pink snout stuffed through the wire fence. The babies, sensing her presence, wiggled in their arms.

"Eieee!" they screeched. Their momma grunted and pressed against the fence anxious to check on them. The girls were quick to reassure the worried pig.

"Sh-h-h, we're just visiting. You'll be back together again to-morrow," Sky said.

"No, we have to keep them apart," Diana said. "She weighs over 450 pounds and could accidentally sit on one. It's not a pretty sight! They're separated about six weeks from birth."

"When did you decide on your project?" Alex asked.

"I started preparing the momma for show as soon as she was born. Her litter of fourteen is one part of this year's. Another is the "creep" I built in our yard," Diana was proud to add. "It's a fenced-in area the hogs can't enter. Wooden slats are set so only the piglets can get in for water and grain. Afterwards, they can run back out to root in the dirt to their hearts content."

Sky and Alex moved on to a building decorated with millions of tiny white running lights and known as the cow palace. There they found prize stock including huge Hereford and Angus bulls and different breeds of milk cows. A lean-bodied red-and-white Ayrshire's collar displayed a first place ribbon. Her leggy calf peeked from under her neck, curious about the visitors. The girls couldn't help chuckling at the sight of the little one sporting a tiny version of its mother's award.

"It's a winner, too!" Alex said.

"This kind is known for its pure-white milk that's excellent for cheese making." Sky read the sign describing the brown Swiss dairy cow.

"Makes me hungry for a chocolate shake and cheeseburger." She patted her tummy.

The large cow, flicked its black tail switch and calmly chewed its cud.

"Where are the bison?" Alex asked an attendant. She directed them to the entire section of the building devoted to that mighty symbol of the American West.

"Before 1850 there were about sixty million buffalo roaming free on the Great Plains," the guide explained. Soon after the westward movement began, their numbers rapidly declined; and by the end of the 1850s there were only five hundred remaining. "Indians followed the migrating herds, depending on the beasts for their livelihood. When the railroads were being built, soldiers and rail workers, some on slow-moving trains, shot them just for sport. Finding it hard to replace their main food source, the Native Americans suffered, and many starved."

"Most slaughtered bison were left to rot in the sun," Sky added, "but the Amerinds never wasted any part of an animal. I think they were our very first recyclers!"

"Onward to the carnival!" Alex said. Tapping her foot, she and Sky sipped a root beer while they waited in the long ticket line for the bumper cars. They finally decided to try the Wild Mouse ride instead. A strong cable between the tracks towed their two-seated car to the top of the roller coaster. They gripped the sides when it whipped down the first of many levels in the maze of steel rails. Made to look like a wind-up mouse, the ride terrified its passengers by sending them to the very edge of a sharply angled corner before making an abrupt turn to rattle downward. Alex and Sky squeezed their eyes shut on the curves and yelled at the top of their lungs.

"That was fun," Sky said. She hiccupped and politely excused herself when a sour bubble burst forth.

"I still taste that soda," she complained after the next ride that whirled them around in a large yellow teacup.

"Let's try the Ferris wheel!" Alex said, skipping ahead.
Up and around they went, enjoying the view until the wheel stopped, suspending them high in the sky while it unloaded passengers.

"Ulph," Sky gulped. Swallowing hard, she began to shiver.

"It's cold up here; I'm sure glad I didn't have a milk shake." She shrank back in her seat when a strong gust swung the gondola.

"Don't turn green on me!" Alex said, catching a glimpse of her face.

"Don't rock the boat," Sky moaned. The wheel lurched as it started moving. She sighed, relieved when it lowered to let off the people seated in front of them.

"We're out next," Alex said, hiding her crossed fingers. The workman pulled the heavy lever, only to spin them for three more revolutions.

"Phew," Sky gasped when her feet touched solid ground again. "I feel terrible," she said on the way back to the campground. Her mother took one look and rushed her inside.

Sky missed the cookout. NanEagle made her hot sugared tea and plain toast to help settle her stomach. She slept through the night, unaware of her parent's concern about their drought-stricken ranch. The weather turned fierce sometime after midnight. Thunder and lightning rolled through in waves, and heavy winds buffeted the huddling vehicles. Scattered rain squalls in the dry storm were no help to the parched land.

Everyone rose early to assess the damage. Groundskeepers were busy cleaning up windfalls and hauling away mounds of debris.

Gramp had left before dawn, heading home to check on the ranch and the hired hands. After eating a bowl of cereal Alex hopped down the steps, happy to find her friend on a lawn chair sketching a beautiful blue spruce tree.

"You must be feeling better! I missed you at dinner," Alex said peeking over her shoulder. "Your work is so good, Sky,

I think you should become an art teacher."

"Thanks." Sky smiled up at her. "You can bet I learned one giant lesson yesterday; it's never to drink root beer again!" she said wrinkling her nose.

"Especially before going on rides that don't include four legs!" Alex teased. "Do you feel good enough to do something this morning? We've tons of time to go hang around the stream."

"Sounds good to me," Sky said with renewed energy.

"Wait a second." Alex hurried inside to search the cupboard for a couple of pie tins.

Yellow aspens interspersed with tall conifers hung low over the sparkling water. A scrawny pine wrapped its roots around an exposed boulder. Sky climbed up on the rock to sit and watch the birds flitting in the forest canopy. She loved the sound of the rushing water. A shaft of silver light caught the red stripe on the side of a rainbow trout. Undulating its way over stones and through ribbons of white water, the fish paused in a quiet eddy to lie in wait for a caddis fly.

Alex meandered upstream, hugging the water's edge searching for the perfect site to pan for gold. Her sneakers lapped up water each time she stepped forward to add a flat stone to the cache in her pockets. Finding a beauty, she sent it skimming sideways, hoping for more than a few feeble hops. Success! Five quick circles spread out with each plop of her missile until it sank out of sight.

"What a beautiful day!" she sang, pausing to inhale the clean air, enjoying its woodsy smell. She continued around a bend and found a tiny inlet, where she dipped her pan into the water.

"Sky, come on, this is a good spot," Alex called. Her friend soon followed and crouched down nearby.

"I'm going to find a huge nugget!" Skylyn announced. She pushed her pan deep into the stream bed. She freed a twig from a clump of leaf litter and waved it back and forth over the tin.

"Glitter! Glitter!" she chanted, then flicked her wand midstream, satisfied as it began to surf the rapids.

"Ta da!" She hauled up the gravel-laden tin and tipped the water out, soaking her jeans.

"Nothing! Phooey!"

As Alex worked her claim an idea formed. She was quick to abandon the pan.

"This is now an official hunt for arrowheads," she declared. Sharp black eyes watched her work a river stone out of its shallow bed, muddying the water. The same dark orbs saw her surprise a nest of fat sandbugs, who dashed away to find temporary quarters. She rolled the rock aside. When the murk had cleared, a transparent stone caught her notice. She unearthed it from the cold sand.

"A piece of rock quartz." Alex turned the smooth mineral over, rubbing each of its glassy, six-sided faces, and rinsed it. She gave it to Sky, who held it up to enjoy the shower of sunlight that pierced it, probably for the first time in the eons it had lain hidden in the stream.

"You're right. There's a large collection on our science shelves."

Alex carefully replaced it, content to think it would continue to while away the ages, a secret earthen treasure safe beneath its cover.

They stepped onto the bank and waited for the insects to reclaim their lodging. Perched quite near and unknown to the busy prospectors, a disappointed ash-throated flycatcher had been patiently watching their every move from a thicket. The small bird had hoped to make a quick breakfast of the homeless bugs.
It flew off to search for easy pickings elsewhere.

They wandered along the shoreline until Skylyn's mother caught up with them. She chose a grassy seat on a sunny part of the bank.

"What have you been doing?" Sky asked when they sat with her.

"I went to the live-stock show and bought a pair of prize-winning Kashmir goats from a nice young man. They'll be delivered next week."

95

"Neat, Mom, I can't wait! I bet the guy who raised them hates to see them go after all of this time. They become pets so quickly."

"Are you planning to weave something special with the fiber?" Alex asked.

"Yes, it's valuable, and will make a beautiful shawl."

"That would be a nice Christmas gift for NanEagle," Sky said. Aggie agreed.

They followed a well-worn trail back to camp, shuffling through wads of damp autumn leaves. Two anglers in waterproof high-tops stood in the cold stream. They skillfully flicked their rods back and forth, letting the hand-tied flies settle gently on the surface, daring a hungry fish to take a bite.

"Remember, it's catch and release, Dad!" Sky reminded him of the stream rules. "I saw a huge trout earlier, but I'm keeping that spot a secret."

"Better tell if you want dinner."

"Nope, my lips are sealed." Turning away she grabbed Tyler to give him a pickaback ride, enjoying his squeals of delight.

Anne sat on a chair next to Sky's grandmother, both content to watch the twins play. Alex caught Chandler and swung him around. She stopped to empty her pockets, counting out each pebble with him, teaching him to pile them into a pyramid.

"I'll show you how to skip stones when they're done fishing," she promised. "We don't want to scare the trout."

Everyone, Sky included, feasted on leftover barbecue before setting off for the arena, hoping Gramp would make it back for finals.

Excitement ran high at the team roping event, when the steer in a center pen and ropers in boxes on each side exited at the same time. As the "header," Rob first lassoed its horns, and Linc, the "heeler," snagged its hind legs, holding steady for the required six seconds. And they won!

The event is always a popular one, recalling the spring and fall roundups when cattlemen moved their herds to different pastures, checked for brands, and gave vaccinations.

With the roping over Steven relaxed in his seat. He sipped a soda and had just reached for a handful of potato chips when the cellular phone rang.

"What!" he yelled. Everyone turned to look.

Fire!

Joseph followed Steven down the highway for an hour until they came to the turnoff for Coyote Ranch. With a toot and a wave, he was gone. The occupants of both RV's rode on in silence, their minds boiling with questions.

"Dad?" Skylyn moved up front and slipped into the empty passenger seat. "Where do you think Taggart is?"

"I don't know," he said, glancing at his side mirror. "I'm sure he's safe. He's still in training, so he won't be on the front line," he reassured her.

"Did lightning start the fires?" she asked.

"Gramp Tanner said it was the same storm that passed over us last night. It's the bone-dry underbrush and pine needles. Toss in wind and lightning, and that's all it takes."

"How long till we're home?" she asked

"Another hour or so," he said stepping harder on the gas. "There's a herd of mule deer over there," her dad announced. "Keep your eyes open; you'll probably see other animals."

"I guess they're moving out just like we might have to do," she said.

"Stop worrying, honey. Instinct has guided them up here to safety already. They know how to take care of themselves."

"I just hope Tag does." She sighed.

Forty minutes from home, they began scanning the countryside.

"Smoke!" Joseph was the first to sight it. "In the mountains southwest of our place, heading north for the runoff dip, I think." He peered out, trying to get his bearings. "About twenty miles away from the ranch as the crow flies, near as I can tell.

"It still a worry," he warned. "Wind's picking up."

When at last they pulled onto the ranch's long driveway. Sky hopped out to open the gate.

"Leave it open in case the fire trucks need to get in," he told her.

They all piled out at once. Strudel and Shep greeted them, jumping up, demanding attention.

"I smell it," Sky said. With the dogs not far behind she and her dad ran to check on the sheep.

Aggie dashed inside to get phone messages and call the fire center for an update. NanEagle hurried home

"The horses are bedded down," John, the shepherd, said, when Raven appeared at the stable door.

"Have you heard from my brother?" she asked. His lips thinned, and he shook his head. Head down, she turned away.

"Do you want help getting the trucks gassed up?" Joseph asked. "Oh, I never should have left," he muttered, running his fingers through his hair.

"Calm down; all the preliminary work is done," John assured him. The animals, too, needed calming. They stamped restlessly in their stalls with their senses operating in overdrive.

"Steven Tanner's offered his ranch if we have to evacuate," Joseph said. "Rob's taking Nambe there tonight in the van."

On South Mountain the fires built in intensity, spurred on by hot winds from the west. Diesel engines whined as huge bulldozers slashed a crude trail up the mountain followed by yellow pumper trucks grinding their way along the rim of the gorge. Fire men and women in protective clothing walked ahead, hacking at the thick scrub. Higher up, they could see pitch-black smoke tinged with orange-red. The surrounding brush and pinyon pines were perfect fodder for hungry flames.

"Name's Jim Goddard, son." A gray-haired veteran held out his hand to the young man beside him. "I guess we're partners. I'm usually at a desk, but they needed everyone on board."

"Taggart Eaglefeather. I'm glad to work with you."

"I'm retiring at the end of this month, and in all my years on the force I've grown to admire Indian firefighters. They do the job best because of their knowledge of the land. And they're not afraid of heights. Big-city fire departments and construction companies love them. I hear they can walk the iron beams on the top of a skyscraper with their eyes closed." Tag merely shook his head and laughed.

"Not me! I'm a country guy not into that stuff."

"Where's your home?" Jim asked as they worked. Tag lowered his machete and pointed.

"Our ranch is about twenty miles northeast of here." The oldtimer nodded.

"What're you raising?"

"Mostly churro sheep and some goats. We have horses and we board some, but the sheep are my dad's hobby and his greatest love. It must run in his Navajo blood." He raised his head and swallowed hard, remembering the comforting sight of grazing flocks. He could almost see the strands of fluffy wool caught on the fences and twigs, blowing in the soft breeze. "Such a waste!" his grandma griped. "There's more than enough for a warm sweater!" She always begged them to gather it.

"Dad's an architect," Tag went on, "and Mom is an artist. She has a studio-gallery in town and weaves churro wool and mohair.

Her work is wonderful." He paused, turning to gaze toward home. "They're away for the weekend. I sure hope they got my message."

"Don't worry, we'll keep ahead of it; they'll be okay."

"Tag called!" Aggie shouted as she ran. "He's over there." She pointed a shaky finger at the mountain, and her voice wobbled. "He says not to worry. We're to keep up on the news and take care of ourselves," she finished with tears shimmering. Joseph hugged her.

Raven ran back to the house just to hear the sound of her brother's voice. Sky took off after her.

Day two dawned as the fire ate its way up the ridge and into what was called the water trough or runoff. From there it jumped the chasm and headed northeast.

Planes loaded with foam fire-retardant, called slurry, dropped their chemicals with as much precision as the gale force winds permitted. In trip after trip helicopters attempted to douse the inferno with water scooped from reservoirs and ponds miles away. Ground pumpers sprayed until they ran dry, leaving the fire to feed its terrible hunger. Soon acres of pines would find searing flames soaring up their trunks and jumping from crown to crown. When the thick sap reached boiling point the trees would burst like fireworks. Forest wildlife in large numbers headed for safer territory. With school closed Skylyn kept watch and prayed for the firefighters and the people on neighboring ranches. She helped her dad and John load up the livestock. Unhappy hens and roosters, already in shipping crates, went next. The horses would be the last to go.

"I'll feel better getting them out of here today," her dad had said earlier that morning.

Sky sat on the knoll behind the barn, absently scratching Strudel's ears. Her bags waited, packed and ready to leave for Alexandra's at a moment's notice.

"I don't like this one bit, pup," she said sniffing the acrid tang in the air. "I bet we'd be safe in our sod barn. Those old sodbusters

101

knew it all. They survived the wild prairie fires that passed right over their heads." Strudel gave her a sloppy lick in answer.

"Another deer," she murmured, watching it cross the pasture and start down the dirt lane. "Uh oh, it looks hurt."

"Nan!" she called. They confined the poodle and set off. They found the animal resting under a scrub oak.

"I can't tell if it's lame or has been burned," NanEagle said. "Looks like an older stag, so it might be a straggler. Let him rest a while, and I'll try to check on him."

Raven and her mother were busy packing pictures and family valuables when Sky returned. She set to work gathering up the woven rugs and wall hangings.

"Mom," Sky said, "I'll be glad when we can put these back."

"Me, too, I just wish we'd hear from your brother. He needs to know we'll be at the Tanners'."

Taggart woke from a four-hour sleep on the bare ground near a temporary base camp. After a welcome cup of coffee he gathered his equipment and hurried up the newly blazed track Heat flicked at his face, and ashes swirled into his nostrils. One after another smoke jumpers exited a circling plane. Their bright parachutes snapped open, and down they glided to land in a clearing with equipment chutes trailing after them.

Reinforcements and firemedics. Good! Tag pictured the grueling task ahead. They'd have to gather up the supplies of food, water, tools, and medicine, their total means of life support. Then they'd set off over treacherous terrain, scrambling to the hotspots, each carrying a heavy backpack.

Brave men and women! The company training film had a good shot of the very efficient lady jumpers. It was too early in the morning for sports! Tag thought. But he secretly wondered if he'd get that assignment someday. His mom would faint if he did.

"Sky," NanEagle reported. "I saw your stag, he's walking okay, but he's still hanging around for some reason. He may be too old to do any long-distance traveling."

"I hope he'll move out if the fire gets close."

Noontime came, bearing unusually high temperatures. Conditions made the area ripe for a dangerous firestorm, an unstoppable killer that could send a huge wall of flames racing across the land with the speed of a tornado.

The Tanner men rolled in late that afternoon, pulling horse trailers. Joseph greeted them, and they set to work. The boarders went first. Because some of them were extremely nervous, Joseph had wrapped their legs to prevent injuries. Sky tossed in sacks of grain and tried to soothe the agitated horses.

"Stay calm guys," she said, stroking each one in turn. "Nambe will be there to greet you." Gramp smiled at her and ruffled her hair.

"You're an old softie just like Alex. They'll be fine," he said. He swung into the cab and pulled out. Both transports headed east.

That evening the quiet seemed to reach every corner and crevice of the house. Sky's parents monitored the CB radio. She and Raven talked quietly, sharing their thoughts about Taggart.

At 4:20 a.m. the order came: evacuate within the hour. Sky's dad called NanEagle and John in his quarters above the stable. They gathered their bags and headed for Aggie's Bronco. Sky clutched a knapsack containing her paints and brushes.

NanEagle came out, gasping for breath in the heavy, choking smoke. Black ashes, remnants of what the fire had consumed, floated in the breeze. Ready to land among rusty leaves or on a thirsty field, some bore traces of glowing red at their edges. Outbursts of flame shot high in the air about eight miles south of them.

"Trees," Raven said with a heavy heart. Sky nodded, tears in her eyes.

"They'll grow again," NanEagle said, squeezing their hands. "Some pines only sprout after fire heats the cones and spills out their seeds."

"Yes, but it takes so many years," said Sky. "And what about our home?" she moaned covering her face.

"Houses can be rebuilt. Be positive, girls! A home is wherever a loving family is together, even if it's only a cave! The community will start collecting reforestation funds the way they did after the fire outside of Yellowstone Park," NanEagle said, sitting as tall in her seat as her petite frame would allow. Sky leaned close against her.

Joseph threw in an extra bag of dog food and boosted Strudel and Shep into the back of the truck. John was to drive the camper holding their clothes and assorted cartons. Aggie turned the key to start the parade of vehicles on its eerie odyssey.

"Sky's here." Anne shook Alexandra awake at six o'clock. Alex bounded out of bed, grabbed her robe, and ran downstairs. She found Skylyn curled up on the leather couch in the den. Alex reached for her; Sky sobbed and held on. "Tag," was all she could say.

"It'll be all right; we'll keep busy." Neither saw Alex's mother turn away from the door, her eyes brimming. Joseph drove back to a hilly lookout on the fringes of his ranch to watch.

"You can't go any closer," warned a sheriff's deputy in tight control of any sightseers. "And you have to get out when we say the word!" Joe inquired about his son whenever exhausted workers trudged past, but they had no news. He stayed until midnight.

Morning dawned clear and cool thanks to the heavy rain that came in the night. The whole crew had time for a rest down in the valley, but everyone realized the work wasn't over by any means. They wielded shovels and drove bulldozers sometimes tilted at precarious angles, turning over smoldering hot roots and the cindered skeletons of trees in which fire could spring to life at any minute. Workers arrived from New Mexico, Texas, and California to relieve men who hadn't once left the struggle.

Red flashed by green as the Bronco overtook a poky tractor on the almost-deserted highway. Worry gripped its passengers at the sight of charred trees and stumps next to the road, most still spiraling thin white smoke upward.

"We made it," Joseph Eaglefeather said, pulling in next to Aggie. "It's not too bad! Thank goodness the house and pastures are okay."

Joseph headed for the stables while the women gathered their belongings. John arrived, grinning broadly. Shep wandered down his favorite lane toward the grazing lands, needing to feel solid ground under his paws, but he missed the animals. The sheep would come home tomorrow. Strudel followed him then veered off and headed for a vantage point on the hill near the old soddie.

Though patches of smoke lingered in the arroyos, settled over the mesas, and topped the blackened fields and mountains, all was in good order on the quiet ranch.

Shep gave a sudden warning, calling both men. He ran toward the scorched south woods beyond the field, still barking for all he was worth.

"What's he after?" Joseph asked. "I don't see any flare-ups, but look! Something's moving in the trees out there.
Good grief!" He turned only long enough to yell across the field, "Aggie! Everyone! Get out here!" They saw him waving and began to run. There in the hazy gray distance, struggling through the charred remains of the forest was a very tired and hungry firefighter named Taggart Eaglefeather. Shep, his furry backside waggling furiously, was the first to greet him.

Aggie ran, forever it seemed, tears streaming down her face. She hugged her son, soot and all, tight against her. The rest stood around grinning. John went off to get the truck, declaring such a hero shouldn't have to walk another step!

Later, Tag told them how he'd dreamed of NanEagle's cornbread and homemade chili, all washed down with cold iced tea. Nan promised to make good on it as quickly as possible. Just then Strudel set up a howl that would have put the henhouse residents to flight. He kept at it.

"Now what's his problem!" Joseph said. "I'd better find out."

"I'll go with you," Skylyn offered. They found Strudle frozen to a spot near the sod barn entrance, still yipping. Approaching stealthily and staying close to the wall, they had almost reached the opening when something clanked against the door. Out poked the handsome set of antlers belonging to a long-legged stag that darted past the startled poodle and disappeared over the knoll.

"Well, I'll be!" said Joseph. "He must have taken refuge in there. I'll bet he snacked on NanEagle's stored apples. What a smart animal."

"You know, Dad," Sky said with a twinkle in her eye, "I think his ancestors must have traveled the Great Plains in covered wagons and settled in soddies!" Joseph laughed along with a very happy Skylyn.

"This has been some week! But all is well, daughter," he said as arm in arm they walked home.

Shep and Strudel heard the stake-body truck rattling down the lane. They dashed off the porch and ran circles around it when Joseph pulled to a stop, barking enthusiastic greetings.

Skylyn helped pull the steel ramp from under the base of the truck. She and John stood on each side ready to reassure the worried animals as they scrambled down. Joseph climbed in among them to urge them on. Unsure of the steep, slippery surface, his favorite goat paused at the top.

"Come on, Dorothy," he said to the bell nanny as he pushed his way through the flock. "Do your job!" he urged, patting her back.

Dorothy made her decision. Carefully testing with one hoof then another, she gingerly picked her way down the ramp. Next a few sheep stepped forward at the sound of her tinkling bell. Reaching the bottom, Dorothy shook out her matted coat, took stock of her surroundings, and made a beeline for the pen. The rest of the woolly crowd quickly followed her lead. Sky called Raven to help, and together they got them settled in, scattering feed to offset the lack of natural pasturage.

Joseph and John headed back to the Tanner ranch for the rest of the livestock. Raven and Sky filled water troughs; Aggie added extra oats to the horses' feed. Skylyn carefully loosened the wire fastening on the crate of Taggart's pet bantam rooster, Barney, and his mate, Wilma. They and their family of chicks as well as Rocky and the rest of the egg-laying crowd scurried from their wooden carriers, happy to roam the home acreage once again. Rewarded with several scoops of cracked corn, Barney strode about, stopping to peck at the tasty yellow kernels. Satisfied, he lifted his head, puffed up his beautiful green-and-black satin chest, and issued a loud "cock-a-doodle-do."

"Barney," Raven said, "you're little but noisy." Without a backward glance, the small fowl strutted off to find some shade under a willow tree, his tail feathers swaying with each step. By twilight, with all of the animals contentedly in their quarters, the Coyote Ranch population had resumed its familiar routine.

The River

Joseph yanked open the Bronco's door and stepped up to check the straps securing the canoe to its top.

"Ready?"

"Ready spaghetti!" Sky answered when her dad slid into his seat. She was delighted at the prospect of a weekend's camping by the Arkansas river with the Tanners.

"Will you stop that silly talk!" the usually quiet Raven demanded, glaring at her. "I'm sick of it." Sky turned to look at her sister.

"Well, crabby, what's your problem? And what are you doing here anyway? You hate this kind of outing!"

"Huh!" the eighteen-year-old said, looking away with her nose in the air.

"Wait a minute," Sky said. "I get it—you think Rob's gonna be there with the Tanners. Well, my lady, here's a news flash: He's working!"

"Mom!" Raven cried. "Keep her quiet!"

"Girls," Aggie said, "we're on vacation, and after the past ten days we need it. No squabbling allowed."

They met up with the Tanners at the Riverview Campground. The men strolled into the tiny office and paid their fees, pausing to chat with the owner for a few minutes. Sky and Alex were glad to be together again.

The twins, with Anne watching, had already found a rope swing hanging from a thick tree limb.

"Dad," asked Sky, "want help setting up the tents?"

"No, thanks," he said. "You girls go have fun. Take you time and explore the river; we'll manage just fine."

"Be back by noon," Aggie instructed.

Raven, Skylyn, and Alex started off through a splendid grove of white birch ablaze with yellow and bronze.

"Indian summer," Raven said. "I love it; warm weather for a little while longer and more time to enjoy the beautiful leaves."

They waded among the rocks and happily called out to people floating by in rubber rafts.

"Fourteen so far." Alex kept count from her seat on a boulder as another appeared around the bend upriver.

The rafters took advantage of the calm, four-mile stretch of river to stir up some excitement. Shouting and screaming they doused each other with water dipped up in bailing buckets. Some brave souls jumped in to swim beside the slow-moving craft.

"I can't wait to canoe along here!" Sky said squelching along in the wet river silt.

"Me too," Raven agreed. She looked at her watch. "I don't know about you, but right now my stomach's growling. It's time to head back."

Trudging upstream along the rocky trail, they rounded a sharp bend near the camp. Sky decided to take a shortcut up the steep bank. She dug her toes into the mud and grabbed a projecting rock to haul herself up and over the top.

"I don't believe it!" She took off running while Raven and Alex were still struggling to follow.

"What is it?" Alex yelled.

"Is it a snake?" Raven screamed. She stopped climbing and hugged the muddy bank. Alexandra grabbed a twisted cedar root and scrambled past her to reach the path.

"Look at that! C'mon Rave, hurry up!" She gave her a tug and dashed off.

"Oh, what have they done now? I hope no one I know sees us!" Raven grumbled as she looked toward the camp.

Sky arrived with Alex not far behind. A group of curious on-lookers hovered nearby.

"Mom! Dad!" Sky shouted. "Whose are these?"

"Surprise!" Their parents popped out of two of the largest white tepees the girls had ever seen.

"They're for us!" the twins announced as they wiggled out from under the canvas.

"Cool!" Alex said. She went through the opening to check the interior. Sky just stared until at last she, too, stepped in. Emerging, she raced around both dwellings.

"I wish NanEagle could see them! I just can't believe it!" she said. "Where did they come from?"

"Joseph and I heard about a man who rents them," Steven answered. "He comes out and sets up anywhere you want."

"Wow!" Alex cried, poking her head out. "Rent-a-Tepee! That's some kind of business! Why did you do it?" she asked.

"Well, we know a couple of girls who have a great love of the outdoors and of American history," Stephen said.

"Not to mention that they've all been a tremendous help lately," added Joseph. "So this is their reward." Skylyn flung her arms around her father.

"Thanks," she whispered to both her parents.

Raven arrived and peered inside. "It's bright, and look how much space it has!" she said, moving through the entrance with Sky following.

"Now I have plenty of room to spread out my painting gear," Sky said. She was quick to notice how lovely the pale canvas looked against the age-darkened lodgepoles and just had to make a sketch of it. She rooted in her backpack, anxious to get started.

"Keep your junk on your own side," her sister warned.

After lunch the girls helped make a fire pit.

"More rocks coming up!" exclaimed Alexandra as she lugged one up the bank to line the hole. Raven and the boys scouted the woods for flat stones to set the metal grill on.

"Chandler, that stone's too small," Raven said. "We need bigger ones." Chan nodded and thrust it into his pocket. Tyler was doing the same.

"Boys, you're loaded down; you must weigh a ton. Why are you saving those?"

"For skipping stones. Alex taught us!" they proclaimed, jiggling their pockets.

"Ah, now I understand," she said with a smile, steering them back toward the campsite. "Well, let's head for the river and try them out."

"All right!" Amid whoops and hollers, they took off running.

"Ready to launch!" shouted Steven. "Everyone have a life vest on? Okay! Give us a push, Anne."

Alexandra's mother threw her deck shoes into the canoe. With one foot in the bow, and the other in the shallow water, she gave a hearty shove and hopped in. The canoe bobbed and danced as she wiggled around to get settled.

"Wooo-eee, Ma!" cheered Alex from her seat next to Skylyn in the Eaglefeather canoe. "Rock and roll!"

Raven, riding with the Tanners to help watch the twins, couldn't stop grinning. She held tight to the wide-eyed boys as they swayed with the motion of the rocking boat.

"Honey, we'll be seasick before we even get started!" Steven teased. Anne merely smiled and reached for her paddle to help send them downstream.

Sky's mother did the honors for their craft. She gave a push that sent them directly into the moving current—with one minor problem: she wasn't in the boat! Slipping on the moss-covered rock, she did a perfect belly flop into the water. She popped up coughing and sputtering.

"That's a ten!" shouted Joseph, working to slow the canoe and draw it sideways to the shore to pick up their errant passenger. Between fits of giggling, Sky and Alex helped her climb in.

"Great dive, Mom." Sky said. "You're Olympic material for sure!"

"You okay? Mrs. E.?" Alexandra asked, handing her a towel from under her seat.

"Guess I'm out of practice," she said, mopping at the clothes plastered to her body. Joseph only snorted.

Cruising slowly downstream, Steven led the way. He pointed out an animal path along the water's edge where the river narrowed.

"Do they get a drink there, Dad?" Chandler asked. His father nodded.

"It's worn quite deep, so it's probably a popular crossing spot, too," he explained. "They always want the greener grass on the other side."

"I see tracks in the mud," Alex said. "Looks like deer have visited recently."

"Mule deer," Joseph told her, drawing their canoe close to the shore for a better look. "And I think some cougar prints."

"Oh," Sky said. "I hope they weren't here at the same time; that's trouble for the mulies."

"There's no sign of a fight. The mud's not churned up," Joseph said.

"I know, but those big cats could stalk the deer," Sky said with a shiver, hating even to think about it.

A beautiful sight greeted them downstream as they drifted around a wide curve. A family of Canada geese was paddling peacefully in the quiet water. Just like their momma, eight goslings dipped their long necks to search for tender aquatic vegetation. Resigned to human intrusion, the geese swam close to the shore and stared at them as they glided past. The poppa, busy preening his feathers on the bank, stopped to keep a careful watch over his family.

"It's a good idea to respect their habitat and try not to disturb them," Joseph said.

"I can't imagine what the animals and birds think of us all," Alex said. "Seems like the traffic would be too much for them."

"Rapids ahead!" Joseph warned. "They look big, but there's a channel through them. We'll have to backpaddle to get in position!" he instructed. "It'll slow us down and we'll shoot them clean! Follow me!" he said as the sound of the rushing whitewater rose.

"Showtime!" Aggie was the first to face the rapids and began to concentrate on her share of the steering.

"Yee-haw! Here we go!" shouted Alex. They rode the ruffled water, broke through, and shot ahead.

"Hang on kids!" Anne told them. "It's a wild roller coaster ride!"

"Woowee! It's cold!" Sky yelled when the spray hit her face. "Feels great!"

"Let's do it again," the boys begged.

High overhead a red-tailed hawk soaring on a sun-warmed thermal looked for a small rodent or a slithery snake. It caught sight of the river runners and decided to ride the rising air current to a nearby mountain for its next meal.

Drifting along, they noticed that the water was running more smoothly and had become darker. They soon got a glimpse of tall canyon walls looming ahead as they neared the end of a long S-curve. Entering the gorge, they saw the yellow bars of afternoon sun that skimmed the mesa rim, hit the wall, and bounced off the sides. As if on cue, the perfectly timed brilliance illuminated vivid slashes of brown cascading down the sand-colored cliffs. Over many thousands of years, the mineral-laden runoff from spring and summer rains had painted them in long, dark ribbons.

"Desert varnish," Aggie said. "I'd love to weave that tone into a rug. It would be fabulous!" Her echo could only agree.

"Look way up there on the edges and overhangs," Joseph told the group as they coasted along.

"I don't see anything," Skylyn said. Her mother passed back the binoculars for the girls to share.

"Yes; I see bumpy-looking things stuck up there, they're familiar, but...hey!" Alex grabbed the binoculars.

"I bet they're swallow nests!" she said. "We have them in the barns. Gramp leaves a window open for them in the spring. The nests are made of mud, and goodness knows there's lots of it around here."

"You've got it!" said Joseph. "It's a colony of cliff and barn swallows; home to hundreds of them, living side by side."

"Well, I've got news," Sky announced, now back in command of the binoculars. "The colonists aren't at home!" She scanned the creative housing made of small, clay pellets plastered on the cliff walls.

"They've gone south for the winter to get a suntan in the tropics!" Aggie quipped.

"Look at that!" Alex said. "Those clever buggers have made little adobe roofs on the nests. Our barn swallows don't need them."

The crews' paddles lay at rest across their knees as they drifted, reluctant to leave the silent bird sanctuary, enjoying the stunning beauty of the golden canyon, and for a brief second of time, becoming a small part of it.

"I've one more special thing to show you," Joseph said, applying power to his paddle. "Then we've got to get going."
Just before the canyon's exit he signaled his wife to halt.
She held them firm, and once again he pointed upward.

"Take a look at the stone's undercut about four feet down from the top." All eyes searched the cliff.

"I see an opening," Raven said. "It looks like a small cave with something round in it."

"You've got good eyes, Rave," her dad said.

"I found it, too!" Sky cried. "So who made it and how'd they get there to do it?" Forgetting where she was, she rocked the boat; both her parents' paddles flew out to steady it.

"It's a storage holder called a *cist*, better known as a *granary*. Does that give you a hint, girls? Think about it and tell us." He threw the question back to them.

"Ancient Indians, of course!" Alex was first to guess. Joseph grinned at her and nodded. "And?" he urged.

"Thinking!"

Sky squinted up at it. "Let's see, they used natural hand and toeholds or hacked out their own. Sandstone is soft and wears easily." She looked at her dad to check her reasoning. "Maybe the holds are there, and we just can't see them."

"Good, Sky!" Joseph said. "If you look closely with the binoculars you'll see that they could make their way from the top left, moving sideways across the cliff's face. Holding on to those small ledges and using a series of chiseled holds would take them directly to the opening. It's very much like what today's rock climbers would do."

"And think of the special gear—shoes and ropes they use," Steven added. "Indians had none of those things, and fear didn't stop them."

"When I was young my father and I made this trip many times," Joseph continued. "He noticed that the wall had patches of greenery sticking out of it, suggesting the presence of tiny cracks. That was enough for the Indians, who knew their terrain. We searched with our eyes and there was the cave!"

"What's inside of the holder?" Tyler asked.

"Food." Joseph said. "Corn, grain, maybe even sunflower seeds, and dried berries!"

Granaries, he went on to explain, were put in out-of-the-way places to be used if someone traveled from camp for more than a day or when enemies caused them to flee from their homes.

"Every Indian knew where one was located. And if not," Joseph said, "they knew enough to use patience and study the rocks for answers. They would soon figure it out, just the way my father did. It's good old common sense."

"Great idea, huh?" Aggie said looking back at the girls. "It must have saved many lives."

"Storage sheds of yesteryear—sort of like Gramp's tool shed," Alex's mother added. "He couldn't live without it."

"But, I don't think he'd enjoy the climb!" Raven teased.

"How did they store the grain?" Sky asked.

"They probably started out with baskets hurriedly constructed of twigs or vines. To make more permanent bins, they covered them with mud that dried and hardened into adobe. Fitted woven lids or simple rock slabs covered them to keep the critters out."

With long shadows now sliding over the tufts of dried grasses and weathered brittle-bush cradled in the crevices, the cliff face took on mysterious textures that created perfect hiding places for myriads of tiny creatures—scorpions, beetles, and spiders.

"Just add water!" Joseph said. Puzzled, they looked his way. "To the grain," he explained. "If they carried it in from the natural holes and depressions on the mesa top and brought in a few sticks of wood to make a small cooking fire, they were set for the night."

He inclined his head, drifting, letting time spin backward, allowing memories of his ancestors to flood his mind in the profound silence. Overhead, a great horned owl, wings spread wide, slipped past with hardly a whisper. It chose a gnarled gray branch jutting from the cliff for its perch, an ideal place to watch for prey it had wisely learned.

A fly buzzed past Aggie's nose, and the ever-present mosquitoes hummed around the girls' ears. The boys looked startled when a fish tail flipped the water. The sound drew Joseph's eyes to the widening circle. He sighed and stirred, taking up his paddle.

"It's late, and we've a way to go before our exit point," he warned.

"I don't want to leave," said Chandler.

"If we don't," Joseph told him, "you wouldn't like going through Brown's Canyon at the end."

"Why?" they asked in unison.

"Do names like, "Razor Rock, Raft Ripper, and Pinball Game give you a clue?"

"Yes! Let's do it!" cried Alex and Sky.

"No!" said the adults. "It's home to the tepees!"

The twins clapped their hands as they remembered the treat to come.

The paddlers dug in with full muscle power. Loving the burst of speed and the wind in their hair, their passengers quickly picked up their rhythm.

"Stroke, stroke!" one canoe sang out.

"Pull, pull!" the other answered.

"It's a race to the finish, ladies and gentlemen!" Sky became the announcer. At last the tired but happy travelers caught a glimpse of the take-out place. They aimed the bows into the sandy shoreline and came to a grinding halt.

"We did it, thanks to our great moms and dads!" The kids congratulated their parents.

"You're welcome, but playtime's over," Steven said. "We need all hands to pitch in before dark."

Everyone helped to load the gear into the waiting 4x4s parked there earlier with help from the camp manager. The canoes were soon secured on top, ready for the drive back.

After a short nap, the boys woke to the smell of hot dogs and burgers sizzling on the grill in the charcoal pit. Coffee boiled in a blue enamelware pot perched on a stone near the edge. Alex's grandfather had rescued it from an old chuckwagon used at the ranch where he worked as a young cowhand.

"Gramp spent a long time yesterday searching for it in the sod barn," Steven said, "and he scoured it clean for our outing. While he scrubbed I heard some more of his stories about the good times they had around the campfires during roundups. He had fun reminiscing, and I very much enjoyed listening."

"Coffee, anyone?" Anne inquired after supper. "I've got baked apples, or we can roast marshmallows and make s'mores for dessert." Votes for some of each carried the group.

By lantern light Skylyn fixed her bedding on the tepee's canvas flooring. She unfolded the new blanket, a gift from her parents, that sported a handsome modern elk-antler design.

"Mom, thanks again, I really love it," Sky said running her hands over the smooth coverlet. She jumped up, wrapped it about her shoulders, and strutted around to model it. "I am the chief!" she chanted.

"I'm glad you like it. Dad and I couldn't have done without either of you last week, that's for sure. Aggie surprised Skylyn by unwrapping a bundle of white tissue paper to reveal two of her own handloomed rugs, which she tossed to the floor.

"Adding local color— they're made from Eaglefeather wool!" she declared. "And I'm not done yet."

Hauling up a large drawstring bag she pulled out one of NanEagle's burden baskets and a small drum. She found a pro-truding knot on the pole near Sky's bed and hung the container on it. "This is for you, compliments of NanEagle," she said. She set the drum on the floor by Raven's spot.

"Mom, I can't believe Dad let you tote along all of this stuff!"

"We both wanted you to experience some of what your grandmother enjoyed as she grew up," she said hugging her young-est daughter, who by then had tears glistening in her eyes.

"It's wonderful," came Sky's muffled reply as she held her mother tight.

"Tanner Tepee" the cardboard sign hanging from a crooked stick proclaimed when the flashlight illumined it.

"Knock-knock!" Sky sang out, and Alex opened the flap.

"I love your sign!" Skylyn said.

"You couldn't find the doorbell?" Alex asked as they dissolved into laughter.

"I've come to invite you to our humble dwelling to see what my mother has done," Sky said.

"Come in here first," Alex invited with a sweep of her arm. She and the twins proudly showed off three of Gramp Tanner's large collection of Navajo rugs, each were pinned high on the canvas sides. A Sioux hide shield, painted and decorated with long tufts of horse-hair, was tied to one of the poles.

"It's great! My mom did the same thing!" Sky exclaimed.

"Uh-huh, they talked." Alex said.

"I should have known!"

Sunday morning the two families gathered around the fire Joseph started with dried twigs the twins had collected. The old coffee pot was steaming away, and Joseph kept busy flipping pancakes on the griddle. Maple syrup sat warming nearby in a heavy crockery pitcher.

"Hotcakes on the line," he announced every few minutes. Plates appeared like magic, and he neatly slid the fluffy brown disks onto them. Aggie made chocolate chip faces on them as they cooked.

"Bacon's up next," Joseph announced. The boys moved as close to the firepit as their mother allowed, so they'd be served first.

"How'd everyone sleep?" Steven asked.

"Like a baby," Tyler declared, eagerly repeating the phrase he'd heard from Gramp so many times.

"I'm going to save my allowance to buy a tepee for our back yard," Alexandra declared.

"Since she won't give it to me, I'm saving some money to buy Skylyn's fabulous drawing of the tepee's interior," Raven said. Taking it from Sky's sketch pad, she held it up and heard her sister's gasp. Everyone gathered around for a better look. Sky lowered her head to hide her red face.

"It's wonderful, Sky," her mother said. "I'll frame it for you if you like. You should think about entering it in the art fair." Sky loved the idea and found Alex at her side murmuring agreement.

Later the men assembled their fishing rods and waded along the stream. Sky and Alexandra followed, hoping to get to cast a line at least once. No such luck.

"Try us later," Steven suggested.

They wandered back to camp and talked the others into a walk along the river bank. On the way they stopped to show the twins a school of minnows in a small eddy. Anne allowed them to scoop a few into their plastic pail.

"Baby minnows are called fry," she told them. "I think these are young fingerling trout. See? They're the size of my finger. They have brown spots and are probably about three months old."

"May we take them home and buy a fishbowl?" they asked.

"How do you think they would feel about not growing up in their beautiful river?" Both stared into the yellow container as the captives bumped their tiny noses against the unfamiliar sides.

"They don't have very much room to swim in there, Chan," said Tyler. "I wouldn't like to live in a small glass bowl."

"Me either. I think the river's better," Chandler confided to him. "Then they'll always be with their brothers and sisters, just like us." They took the bucket to a rock pool and slowly lowered it deep enough to free the fish. Out they swam, right over the top. The boys watched them hurry to greet the others before darting away, happy to get on with the business of the day.

"They're free, Momma," Chan said.

"I'm glad," Ty added with a big sigh.

"Chick-a-dee-dee-dee," came the sound from a black and white bird flitting from branch to branch on the blue-green needles of a Western white pine.

"See," Anne said pointing out the tiny black-capped chickadee. "Even that little guy agrees with your very grown-up decision."

"Can we fish now?" Alex asked her dad.

"Okay," he said. He reeled in his line and waded back to the bank. After changing the fly, he proceeded to instruct them in the art.

"Cast with your forearm." He demonstrated a few times. After a stern warning to watch out for others when backcasting, each had a turn.

"Catch fish, not people!" he said.

Sky went first, casting over and over into a shaded pool. Suddenly she felt a tug and saw a splash.

"Strike!" Steven said. "Pull the line sharply to set the hook. Now reel it in!" She wound as fast as she could, but the uncooperative fish swam away.

"Play along; give it more line," he encouraged. "It'll soon stop." She wound again, and this time it swam toward her. As the fish drew near, Steven bent down with the net and scooped it up.

"It's a brownie!"

"With shaking arms Sky tried to hold the pole still while he pulled it out.

"Wow," he said, "it's a nice size! Good work Sky!" Everyone admired the eight-inch trout.

"Is it okay?" Worried, she watched his every move as he carefully removed the hook.

"Yes, it's fine."

"Can we just let it go?" she asked. Steven nodded, and Sky leaned close, watching as he lowered the brown trout, cupped lightly in his hands, into the stream. Sky saw it disappear in the watery depths.

"Nice work, Sky." Joseph said at her side. "Who's next?" He volunteered his services as teacher.

"Oh, Dad, I didn't know you were here," she said.

"I sure am, and I saw your every move. I think you're great at fly fishing," he said with a grin, handing his rig to Raven.

"Thanks," Sky said. She went to sit on the bank while the other two moved to separate areas for their turns.

"Hello to the fishermen! Whoops, sorry about that— fisherwomen, too!" came the voice of someone working his way through the trees.

"Hi, Rob!" Sky called from her perch on the bank. "What are you doing here?" she asked when the others had greeted him.

"Gramp sent me to check on you campers. I saw your neat accommodations back there; your mother gave me the grand tour.

Looks like fun."

"Hey, Rave, I didn't know you liked to fish. Catch any sharks yet?"

Raven simply shook her head and started to step away. Just then her line took a hit. Oh no, she thought. Please, not right now with Rob watching!

"You've got one! Pull up and set it!" her dad directed. Her pole bent toward the water with the reel screeching as line whizzed out. She caught the spinning handle and cranked it as fast as she could. The fish gathered its strength and took off again. Without a thought to her footwear, she stepped into the stream and felt her way over the rocks to get closer to the action.

"Let it run!" Joseph hustled along the bank with his net, following the line and her every move, shouting instructions. "It's a biggie, and it's running hard! It'll tire quickly."

Raven gave the fish its head. She played along with its every whim, calmly reeling in and letting it pull back out. Steven and Alex dropped everything to follow the battle. Ducking around Joseph, Rob made his way up and down the rock-strewn bank.

"No!" her dad hollered when Rave moved toward the deeper water. "Keep in the shallows!" She pulled her rod to the right and stepped back as the fish dove into the dark water.

"It's okay; pull, then reel!" Raven complied. She tugged, using all her strength. Suddenly the line went slack, and the fish turned to make a run her way. She spun the reel.

"Keep going," Joseph said. "Just keep it going, honey, and for heaven's sake don't lose it."

When Raven drew the tired fish toward her, Rob grabbed Joseph's net and went to dip it out. The huge trout almost filled it.

"It's a cutthroat, at least ten pounds worth!" Rob exclaimed. Joseph waded out to help him remove the hook.

The men gathered around her. "Every fisherman's dream," they gave a collective sigh.

"You've won the prize, honey," her father said. Exhausted,

Raven merely smiled.

"Hold it right there!" came a shout. They all turned, and Aggie snapped a shot of the very happy group.

"Thank goodness someone had a camera," Steven said, "or it would have been just another story of the one that got away."

"We heard the noise and came running. I have it all on tape, too. We wouldn't have missed it for the world! What a gal!" her mother said, beaming proudly at Raven.

"Now can we do as Sky did and let the poor thing go? He deserves his freedom," Raven declared. "He's quite a fighter."

Rob gave the twins a last look at the fish and waded out to set it free.

"I'll give the star fisherwoman a ride home after dinner. I want to learn her secret of fishing for cutties!" Rob told them. Raven was too tired to resist.

"What a day," Joseph murmured, snug in his own bed late that night. "I've fished all my life and never caught a cutthroat that size. Can you imagine? That girl fought like a trouper, and she never complained once. Come to think of it, she never said a word during the whole thing. She's a natural, and Sky will be good at it, too. Just like their dad!"

"I have to agree with you, honey," Aggie mumbled from deep in her pillow. "And I'm sure glad Raven knows better than to just yack, yack, yack!"

Minus Two

"Alex! Over here!" Skylyn waved to her friend when she hopped off the school bus. She gathered up her backpack and rushed to meet her.

"You're back, great!" Alex said. How'd it go in Boulder yesterday?"

"Fine. The University of Colorado is really super. We had fun exploring the area. It's colder up there though. We saw a huge herd of elk roaming in the woods, I couldn't believe it!" she said. "A groundskeeper told us they sometimes wander onto the campus. There's a flock of Canada geese that winters at the local pond, too."

"It sounds great; I could live there! Is Raven all settled in?" Alex asked as they rushed into the building and headed for their classroom.

"Yes. Mom bought her some neat furniture. She's lucky; she also got a new computer; and a desk that weighed a ton," she added. "Dad had to ask someone to help haul it up to her dormitory room. She's on the fourth floor—he says it's in the nosebleed section!" Both chuckled. Sky drew quiet as she searched for an empty hook for her jacket. She then turned to her friend. "I hate it, Al. It seems like she's moved out for good."

"She'll be back for weekends and holiday's. Christmas is right around the corner!"

"I know, but the house is so quiet, and there's no one to pester now, especially at bedtime. I feel funny—like lost or something."

"Gramp says change is part of life," Alex said, "and we have to face it whether we like it or not. I'm just happy that our families are friends because we get to do so many good things together. I hope that never changes."

"Me too," Sky agreed. "I always have fun with you. You're my best buddy. Hey! I have an idea!" Sky brightened. "Let's make a friendship-forever pact."

"Sounds good to me!" Alex said, smiling as they shook on it. "Anyway pal, we've still got some time here; and besides, I'm not ready to tackle junior high yet.

"Not to mention high school or college," Sky added, "although the university was sort of neat..."

Book III

Working Together

Big plans

"Will the Forestry Service ever start replanting South Mountain?" Skylyn asked, stamping her foot on the damp ground. "It looks like a lunar landscape—nothing but trees turned to charcoal skeletons and blackened grazing lands. I'm sick of it! April is only a week away, and the animals and birds have nothing to feed on!" She and her grandmother gazed at the scarred hills still sporting dingy patches of snow.

"Believe it or not, Sky, fires help the grasslands. My father told me the early Indians used controlled fires every ten years or so to renew the soil. They discovered that ashes had nutrients that made them greener than ever. They're Mother Nature's fertilizer!"

Less than two years ago a raging forest fire had threatened the parched southwestern area near the Eaglefeather's Coyote Ranch. They were forced to evacuate, taking the rare Navajo sheep, goats, and boarding horses. Days later the family returned to their Colorado homestead and found the inferno had destroyed thousands of acres, only to be contained at the very edge of their pasture lands.

"If the drought continues, there'll be nothing for them in the hills this summer either, and the flock will be unhappy again."

"All in good time, honey. John's a knowledgeable shepherd. He'll keep watch over the churro as they forage around here, or he'll get permission to graze them elsewhere."

"Well, it's much too slow for me! Seems like they need a wake-up call," Skylyn declared, kneeling to pet Strudel. "What can we do to help get things moving, NanEagle?" Sky asked.

"I haven't read anything about it in quite a while. Why don't you go to that computer you got for Christmas and dig up some information? You're a class officer—talk to your teachers and classmates and get them involved. I remember how your dad and your Uncle Glenn loved community projects. They both were active in student government in junior high."

"Good idea! You always come up with something, Nan. Now how about keeping me company while I feed the animals? Then I'll call Alex, and we'll get busy searching the Internet."

Alexandra, waved good-bye to her dad as she stepped off the running board of his new Ford Explorer. Steven held his breath while she slipped and slid down the school's icy sidewalk. She pushed through the door, hoping to find her friend before the start of their first class.

"Sky!" she spotted her at the end of the hall by the lockers and dashed down the empty corridor to meet her.

"Hi! You're early! Boy am I glad to see you!"

"Dad brought me. I've got tons of money-making ideas. We've got to talk to our homeroom teacher, and the art and social studies teachers," she said, stopping for a moment to catch her breath.

"Great!" Sky said, grabbing Alex's backpack. "I've got a dozen schemes, too. How about a school carnival, candy sales..." Sky gave her a quick rundown. Alex listened as she stashed her jacket and gloves and pulled out fresh gym clothes. Stacking up the books for their morning classes, she added a few more thoughts to her growing list on the way to change for PE class.

"I like your bake-sale idea, Al. Do you think the home-ec teacher would help us organize it?"

"She might. We've time to go over and ask her," Alex replied.

"Mrs. Pierce, maybe our mothers and all your students could make cookies. You know how the boys love the cafeteria's big chocolate chip and sugar ones. We'd have signs to advertise well ahead of time so they can save their money," Alexandra chattered on. "And I'm almost sure the art teacher would donate paper for Skylyn to make posters."

"A cookie sale! That's so cool, Al!" Sky was impressed with her friend's input. "My head's already spinning with designs for the banners," she said as they hurried to the gym.

"Thank goodness Mrs. P. liked it! Step one of our plan is under way," Alex said, clapping her friend on the back.

By the end of the day they'd explained to each of the teachers their fund-raising ideas for replacing the trees in part of the burned-out forest.

"Girls," the social studies teacher reminded them, "I hope you realize it would only be a tiny step toward restoring such a huge area."

"We know that, Mr. Raymond." Alexandra nodded. "But my grandfather always says any journey starts with the first small step. Sky and I intend to make it a giant one!"

"All right, I like your attitude. I'll be glad to help in any way I can, and I'll speak to Principal Edwards for you. Sky, tell me again about your end-of-the-year school carnival..."

Thursday they met Mr. Edwards with an outline of their plan. He promised to set aside time for them to address all three junior high grades the next day.

After his remarks on the office microphone and the salute, to the flag, he introduced Alex. "She has some news about an upcoming event."

"...so we'll be looking forward to Cookie Day in about two weeks." She concluded her announcement with, "Save your allowance to help out our mountain reforestation project. Now, I give you Skylyn Eaglefeather."

Sky told them about the carnival to be held with the help of the PTA. Mr. Edwards grinned as whistles and cheers reverberated through the building.

"My parents have contacted the Forestry Service," Sky continued, "and they've received a promise of ten thousand free pine seedlings that should arrive at the end of May. Any money we take in from the cookies and the carnival will be used to buy extra trees for the overlook." She relayed Joseph Eaglefeather's offer to use their ranch as a command center for the Memorial Day planting.

"Alexandra's father and grandfather, who were once active Eagle Scouts, have invited area scouts to help us. We hope all of you will come with your families. You're welcome to bring tents and stay over that Friday night. I'll give you more news as I get it."

"Next stop, Tanner Ranch!" Charlie the bus driver announced, pulling up at the end of the lane. "I see your grandfather's waiting for you, but I think he's in trouble. Your twin brothers have commandeered the front seat." He laughed when Chandler honked the Jeep's horn, and Tyler waved Gramp's Stetson.

"He's picked up the boys from kindergarten, and now he's baby-sitting for Mom while she bakes." Alex couldn't help chuckling at the sight of him slouched in the back seat of his 4x4. "It looks like he's lost his wheels and his hat," she said.

"Bye, Alex!" the Royce brothers called to her. They pointed to Skylyn's handmade Cookie Day notice taped above a window. "Make them real big!" Alexandra looked back and waved.

"Charlie's saving the front seat tomorrow for cookie baskets," she said. He'd already been promised a bag of goodies.

On the way to work, Aggie dropped off Sky and her precious cargo at the school. Sky thanked her mother and set out for the cafeteria. She was tired but primed and ready when once again she caught sight of her colorful posters. For the past two weeks they'd been plastered everywhere, tantalizing the students' taste buds. With a big smile she handed the PTA president her contribution and headed for her locker.

"Here's the Poster Girl," Alex called out.

"Sky, your art work is so great," Paula Adams, the class secretary said. "I'll miss it when it's taken down."

"I'll save you one," Sky said.

"Sign it for me, please, because I know you'll be a famous artist someday!"

"Students, it's cookie time! As an extra sweet treat, you'll be dismissed fifteen minutes early!" the assistant principal announced at 2:00 p.m. and patiently waited for the noise level to subside. "Head for your buses when the second bell rings!"

Skylyn heard her name mentioned over and over again as she sold baggies of chocolate-chip treats from a pile on her card table. What are they saying about me? she wondered.

"Sky!" Alex rushed over to her. "They loved them! Yours sold out in ten minutes. It was a feeding frenzy at my table, and I had to call for help! We took in thirty-five dollars! You must have worked for hours last night. How did you make those fabulous cookies?"

"Mom and I did it together. She bought new cookie cutters

and did all the baking. I had fun with the colored icing." Relaxing for a second, she looked up at her friend. "I sort of sculpted a special one for you, Al, but it'll have to keep until I'm finished here."

Ten minutes later Alex got to unwrap Sky's gift, an extra large cookie baked in the shape of a horse head—a perfect "hand-painted" replica of Alexandra's Jessie.

"It's much too beautiful to eat! Jessie would be proud!" She reached out to hug her friend. "Thank you. Your creations were the hit of the day! The guys loved the ones shaped like tools, especially the saws and hammers. The flowers on sticks were neat, too. What a gal!"

The girls used the intercom once again on Monday to thank everyone for supporting the event, saying a grand total of $450 had been added to the treasury. Plans were well underway, Alex announced, for the PTA carnival. "It will be held on the last day of school from 5:00 until 10:00 p.m. Lots of parents and teachers have already signed up to help. There will be action-packed booths, rides, and food stands loaded with popcorn, ice cream, soda, and hot dogs."

"Hurry up, Al! I heard some boys are joining, too," Sky said, as they changed into jeans along with classmates Paula Adams, Merry Steel, and other eighth and ninth grade students who were in the archery club.

"I'm so excited, Sky. I'm glad you talked me into it."

"NanEagle's been teasing me about reverting to my roots!" Sky wriggled into her sweatshirt as they made their way out to the field. "But she cautioned me not to give any war whoops!" Miss Brunner had the heavy, straw-filled targets set up and waiting for the start of the newly formed club. She gave a talk on safety and showed how to use the equipment. Her skillful demonstration earned cheers.

"Who's first?" she asked. Several of the older kids stepped up.

"For safety's sake, everyone else stand in the designated area behind them. Stop yackking and pay attention." Groans of disappointment accompanied the first flight of arrows that fell far short of the targets.

"Focus on the bull's eye, and don't be afraid to pull back hard!" The teacher encouraged the shooters, helping them adjust arm position and stance. "Let's let some others try."

Sky and her friends had their turns with the same results. Sky's first arrow hit the ground at the base of the target, and Alex's roamed far to the right. After a few more rounds, Skylyn and Luis seemed to catch on, each nipping the edge of the target.

"Just call me William Tell!" Luis bragged.

Paula had better luck when her arrow struck the circle and stayed put for a few seconds.

"She's Maid Marian!" someone sang out.

"I'm going to do this until I get it right," Alex muttered. She gritted her teeth, pulled the bowstring taut, squinted one eye, and let the arrow fly. It pierced the target's second circle and stuck. About time, she thought.

"We'll name her Robin Hood," Miss Brunner said, joining in the fun. "Everybody will soon get the hang of it—it just takes practice."

"You know, Al," Sky moved next to her and spoke quietly after the instructor moved on, "I just thought of something. Maybe we could get the mountain man we met at the rodeo to come to our carnival and do his tomahawk toss."

"That's a great idea!" Alex's head snapped up. "But how can we find him? We don't even know his name—wait! Maybe we could ask the people who put on the rodeo."

"Dad's picking me up after school, I'll talk to him," Sky whispered. "Ask Gramp, he'll know someone!"

Enjoying a beautiful Easter weekend, Sky and her mother, accompanied by Strudel and Shep, walked to the hilly slopes that fringed their ranch.

"Look, a spot of green meadow grass!" Aggie was happy to

point out the welcome blades squeezing through the earth of the barren fields. "Maybe we'll get lucky and have enough rain for a good growing season. And there's another healthy sign—a tiny pine that's poking through the stump right by your toes," Aggie said to Skylyn, who seemed close to tears at the ruin before them.

"That's good, I agree," Sky said, leaning down to caress the new life. "I'm sorry, Mom, but I miss the spring flowers and all the wildlife."

"There's an old saying, 'what goes around comes around,'" Aggie said, her arm circling Sky's shoulders. "Just be patient; your planting day is only four weeks away. Oh well," she said, "I guess I'll let you in on something I was keeping as a surprise: your sister's coming home from college that weekend, and your brother will be here for all the fun. Raven said she'd help me cook, and Taggart's rounded up a firefighting buddy to work with us."

"Good! I miss them." Sky brightened. "It'll be neat to have so many families camping here." She turned to look back at the pastures. "I forgot to tell you that Susan and Merry are coming with their Girl Scout troop, and Alex and I are sleeping in Paula's tent."

"That sounds like fun! Did I mention that Gramp Tanner's invited the area 4-H Clubs?" Aggie asked. "And Raven said Rob Stanley and his rodeo friend, Lincoln Jesperson, will come over with the Tanners. We'll have tons of help."

Step Two

"Coyote Ranch looks like a real Indian encampment! Just look at the scout flags flying and all the tents!" Alex said to Sky and Raven as she danced around the fire pit her dad, and Gramp were digging near an old deep-water well that still sported a rusty hand pump. It would serve as the campers' source of water for the weekend.

"You two will be happy to know that there's a tepee pitched out there over the hill," Raven said.

"We've been there already, Rave. It belongs to the Clark family, and we helped them erect it!" Sky said. "Getting those eighteen poles up was sort of like playing a giant game of pick-up-sticks!"

"It was a blast!" Alexandra added. "They said we could make designs on it later—Sky's got her paints and brushes ready to go."

Steven looked up as Joseph's truck returned with NanEagle sitting beside him. He'd collected a small load of rocks to line the pit.

"We're almost finished, Joe," Steve called. "I think Gramp's anxious to get the coffee pot on!"

All right, let's do it." He hopped out and walked around to help Nan out. "We went to the overlook for a bird's-eye view of the tents."

"It's seemed like old times," she said, brushing a tear from her cheek. They grew quiet, giving her their full attention. "The sight brings it all back to me. Our tepees were much bigger, though," the Indian woman recalled. "It was something to see, with hundreds of campfires glowing in the evening. I can picture my parents and my sisters gathering round to hear the elders' stories. But the drums were my favorite! The dancers wore feathers in their hair. Bands of leather attached with black deer claws circled their ankles and the tops of their hide boots.

The hollow claws made tinkling sounds as they moved with the pounding beat." She paused, eyes closed for a second. "And," she proudly held up a finger, "all the drummers and dancers knew their parts so well that without a signal, they stopped at the same moment—beaters up! The silence was profound. There was such a wonderful feeling of freedom—all good memories for me." She turned to Joseph. "Thank you, son." He could only nod with glistening eyes.

A distant rattle meant yet another truck was crossing the cattle guard. Joseph shaded his eyes to get a good look.

"I think we've just had our prayers answered," he said. They turned to watch a brown vehicle wind its way toward them, cheering when they realized it was the forest ranger delivering the pine seedlings.

Joseph greeted his old friend, Brad Tully, and introduced him around.

"I'd like you to meet the two young ladies responsible for this wonderful occasion."

"Congratulations!" the ranger said. "Joseph told me all about you. I'm impressed." Sky and Alex glowed at his praise.

Mr. Tully was quickly relieved of his load of fifty white buckets, which were deposited in the sod barn. A small crowd gathered to look at the skinny, foot-long bundles of baby trees.

Sky longed for her lush forest. She bitterly regretted never having put that beloved vista on canvas. Now, staring down at the wispy green tips peeking out from their damp newsprint wrappers, she wondered if such wee living things would ever make a difference on that tarnished hillside. Or would it all be for nothing? Sky lifted a parcel from its temporary home and carefully unwrapped it.

So tiny! As she separated one from its compact nest of siblings, her heart seemed to fly into her throat: what if these babies were too delicate to survive?

"How many are in each bucket?" she asked the ranger.

"Ten per parcel, two hundred trees per container." She gave him a wan smile and darted out of the soddie.

"Two hundred! Right there?" Alexandra moved closer, circling a container with her arms. "I've got a whole, brand new, woodsy grove in my hands!" she sang.

"Nan!" Skylyn thumped onto her grandmother's front porch and tore open the door.

"Honey, calm down and tell me what's going on."

Sky soon took her back to the earthen barn and scooped up a wet bundle, urging her to open it.

"New life," Nan said, pausing to inhale the pine scent already evident in the ancient dwelling. "Wonderful!" She smiled at Skylyn. "They're slim and fragile but very hardy, able to bend and sway with the wind and resist the elements." She removed a tiny slip of a tree. "Look, Granddaughter, at the long, feathery roots, nice healthy symbols of strength and endurance, like what you and Alex have shown with the courage to visualize a project and bring it to life. Because of that, one day soon there will be a wonderful new land for the animals to roam once again."

"Thanks." Sky took a deep breath. "I needed that, Nan," she whispered.

Taggart pulled in at seven o'clock that evening, his pickup truck weighted down with four-foot logs cut from fallen timber. His sisters were happy to see him and to meet his friend, Kip.

"Your furniture order is ready, sir," he said when his dad rushed up to greet them.

"Good deal, Tag! Lots of seating," Joseph said. Unloading the wood, they quickly set to work arranging it in double rows around the campfire. "Just the right touch."

"Don't bet on it, Dad," Raven said. "Mom just might sneak out some of her woven rugs for a decorative accent!"

That evening the workers gathered around the fire to get acquainted over hot drinks and donuts. One of the Scouts played his guitar for a singalong. At last Joseph stood and thanked the volunteers for coming and reviewed tomorrow's schedule

"You're welcome to use the bathroom in the barn, and the well water's pure." He promised to keep the fire stoked for anyone wanting to make a late night snack or a hot breakfast. "Help yourselves to Gramp Tanner's famous cowboy coffee steaming on the grill. Be aware!" Joseph cautioned, grinning. "He makes it just the way they did during the old-time roundups when the camp cook tossed the beans right into the boiling pot."

"Early in the morning," Joe continued, "we'll truck the plants to the edge of the field and start from there. Your team leaders will guide you. Thank heaven the earth is still moist and spongy from the snow melt. Just use a stick; you won't have a hard time punching the holes. Try to keep the plants in line about twenty feet apart and heel them in carefully."

Well before dawn the ranch slowly came alive, quickly revealing a surprise. Snow had fallen during the night, powdering the surrounding fields. Muffled voices from the encampment gently blended with the soft morning sounds from the stable residents and their caretakers.

Shep and Strudel, unused to all of the activity, not to mention the tantalizing smell of bacon and eggs cooking over damp mesquite logs, circled the grill whiffling their noses. Their barks accented the pop and crackle of the wood.

The girls peeked out from a slit in the tent flap, causing a flurry of flakes to dust their noses.

"Whee!" Paula exclaimed, loving the shivery feeling.

"That's a cold wake-up call!" Alex said.

"Snow!" Sky clutched her robe tight to her chest. "The seedlings will freeze to death!"

"Don't worry," Mrs. Adams said. "By the time we have breakfast and get out there it'll be all right."

Sky dressed hurriedly, excused herself, and scurried toward home. She found her dad in the barn feeding the horses.

"Whatever will we do, Dad? It's too cold for the baby plants!" she said, reaching out to stroke her horse's velvety nose, seeking comfort from the gentle-hearted Nambe.

"Morning, honey." Joseph smiled at her. "Ah, worrying already, are we?" He gave her a hug. "Relax—we'll have no doom and gloom today. Did you forget that there is a very strong force soon to be at work out there for us? And I don't mean the volunteers."

"Are you talking about the sun?" she asked, her brow furrowed. Joseph nodded.

"I sure hope you're right." Sky sighed, patting Nambe's neck. She gave her father a tiny smile and made her way outside just as a well-worn station wagon clattered to a stop beside the rough plank door. A pretty red-headed woman wearing a warm coat and a battered straw hat wound down her window and smiled up at her.

"Good morning. I'm Pat Eden, are you Skylyn?" Sky nodded. "I heard about your project, and I'm here to help," she said, climbing out of the car. "You see, I receive a shipment of seedlings to give away each year." She explained how she placed notices in the newspapers and waited at the town library or the shopping center to hand them out to people.

"Every year at this time I distribute five hundred of them in

memory of my son, who was killed by a drunk driver on Memorial Day, 1990. I like to drive around and visit my gift trees. It makes my heart sing to see where they'll be growing. By now, many are six or eight feet tall," she said with pride. "Today I've brought you some native flowering shrubs, and if you can find good places for them I'll be happy."

"Will we ever—that's awesome!" Sky said. "I know how good it must make you feel. I'll be sure to look for your ad next year. But I'm curious, Mrs. Eden. How did you hear about what we're doing?"

"It's in all of the morning papers and on the TV news. Look," she said, pointing her thumb over her shoulder. Sky turned to discover a huge television van with a satellite dish perched on top lumbering down the rutted lane.

"Oh, my word! It's—Channel Nine," she cried. "Dad!" Sky called to him just as Alexandra rounded the corner shouting her name.

Two men converged on them with a microphone and camera. As both sets of parents looked on, the girls reluctantly accepted their fifteen minutes of fame, happy to promote their cause but totally embarrassed at just how awful their hair must look.

An hour later the full work force went scrambling over the hills, digging into the soil and giving new life a chance to flourish. Many sang as they worked; others laughed, calling out to one another, all content to spend a beautiful sunny day outdoors.

High on the overlook, with a view of the ranch below and Buffalo Meadows to the northeast, a group of twelve labored.

"Alexandra," Gramp called. "I need the shovel."

"Coming. I just have to tamp in this little century plant." Finished with her task, she hopped over a bush and handed it to him.

"Gramp," she confided, "you have to see the plantings I've nestled next to a rock. I think they look rather nice; I just might have a new calling. Mom says they're *Apache plume* and are related to the rose family. They have silvery puffs at the tips of their branches after they bloom," she recited. "I'd sure like to come back and see them."

Close by, Alexandra's mother, and Aggie steadied heavy wooden signposts in two newly dug holes while Steven and Joseph filled them in with fresh-mixed cement. "Good work by the Fab Four!" Sky said, admiring the new replacement for the burned ones that had stood for years, offering information to travelers about the magnificent vista.

Long ago on this splendid plain, Sky thought, the ancients must have lingered to watch hungry coyotes or wily wolves nip at the flanks of grazing bison, hoping to spark a stampede and separate a tasty newborn from its momma in the confusion.

"More mulch," came a cry from Rob and Raven as they worked a prairie-seed mixture into the sloping bank near several freshly planted rosettes of blue yucca, whose drooping pods would display creamy white flowers by summer.

"Coming right up," Linc said. "Do you have room for a couple more? I've got a wild rose and some rabbit-foot brush."

"Yes," Rob called. "But we'll need some water; we're running out."

"I see the truck now."

"Busy as a beehive," Sky remarked when she finished setting small rocks along the edge of one of the foot trails.

"Well let's hope the bees take the hint," Alex said, "and resettle here!"

"They will, Al," Gramp said. "I just planted some of their favorite purple clover and Indian paintbrush. The whole place is shaping up just fine. It's amazing what a few hands can do with a great big idea."

"It looks beautiful." Pat Eden stopped working fertilizer into a wildflower bed to lean on her rake handle, savoring the effects of their handiwork. "The girls have given me another good day to celebrate life."

Sawing and hammering away back at the ranch, Tag and Kip had put the finishing touches on the split-log benches they were fashioning into seats and tire stops for visitors to the historic over-

143

look. Everyone greeted them as they pulled in to set them up.

"Thanks for a great job, guys," Steven said. "It spruces up the place and softens that charred look quite a bit."

"Kip's a carpenter in his spare time," Tag said. "He wields a mean hammer; that's why I brought him along! Hey, maybe we should start a rustic furniture business."

"That would be perfect, Tag," Sky chimed in, teasing her brother, "you'll make lots of money when you have a fire sale."

"Okay, time to head back to the others; we're all getting silly," Joseph said.

By late Saturday afternoon, the happy but exhausted volunteers made their way down from the hills. The Eaglefeathers and Tanners offered them a place to wash up, cold drinks, and sandwiches the PTA mothers had delivered.

Standing on the flat side of a leftover log, Principal Edwards, thanked everyone for helping to make the day a success. He invited the two celebrities to come forward.

Sky stepped up onto the log with Alex standing beside her.

"We took a giant step forward today. Our seedlings aren't noticeable—yet!" Sky said, "but they'll soon make a difference. When you drive past the overlook on your way home, be sure to see what our school-fund purchases have made possible and think of what the carnival proceeds will add to it."

"I want to thank Sky," Alex said, taking her turn to speak. "She was tireless in her work on both of our projects, but we're not quite done. We plan to get permission from the Park Service to place a brass plaque at the restored lookout area in appreciation for our new friend, Mrs. Pat Eden. It will be a permanent memorial to her son, Paul."

"You girls entered the real world today—television interviews, addressing a large crowd. You held your own very well," Steven said at the Eaglefeather dinner table later that evening. "We're so proud of you. I'm a bit worried, though— you're not thinking of running for the Senate or House of Representatives, are you?"

"I don't know about Skylyn, Dad, but I plan to be the first woman president of the United States," Alexandra said.

"Me, too!" Skylyn said. "We competed against each other in the rodeo, so I guess we'll be doing it again." She looked at her friend. "But, um-mm, excuse me, Al..., then who will you get to run your campaign?"

Final Plan

"School's out, yay!" shouted a seventh-grade boy dashing to be first on his bus, hoping to get a good seat for the last ride of the school year. Others followed carrying heavy backpacks stuffed with belongings from their now empty lockers.

Pleasantly surprised on this hot June day with a welcome gift from the faculty, the bus drivers gathered earlier than normal to chat at their usual spot on the sidewalk. They were enjoying drinks from the array of sodas nestled in an ice chest along with bags of assorted snacks. A large thank-you banner hung above, inviting them to bring their families and join everyone at the carnival later that day.

"Hey! Look over there!" Luis yelled. It was six minutes before departure time on bus number twenty-five. The students grew quiet when he pointed to a thin trail of dust rising from the edge of the soccer field.

"Who the heck is that?" his friend Wally Chapman shouted.

Alexandra hopped on the first step of the bus to speak to her friend Kim. She was in time to see everyone seated on the right surge to the opposite side for a better look. Alex leaned down to check. In the momentary silence they heard her say,

"Oh, my gosh, I forgot all about him!" They all turned to look at her.

"Who?" someone asked.

"It's Mountain Man on horseback! That's who! And he's got someone with him!" A noise to rival Mt. Saint Helens erupted. In the pandemonium Alex found Kim, shouted something into her ear, and hurried off to search for Sky and her family, who were helping to set up the carnival in the parking lot, soon to become the festive midway.

"Sky!" she cried. "He's here!" Sky turned and looked at her. "He? Who?"

"Who-whoo, are you an owl?" she taunted, "Come on!" Alex demanded, tugging her toward the crowd.

"The Mountain Man has arrived, and you won't believe your eyes," she said. They rushed toward the front of the long line of busses and pushed into the growing crowd. All watched wide-eyed as a rider in coonskin cap, tanned-deerskin shirt, and leggings slowly rode the length of the playing field toward the midway's grassy verge. A bay horse followed, carrying a woman with a beautiful white feather in her plaited black hair. She wore a fringed buckskin dress to match her partner's outfit. Each horse dragged a travois with a pile of tightly lashed bundles on it.

"Wowie! What great publicity for our fair!" Skylyn shouted, now fully aware of the ruckus in the loading zone. Alexandra listened to the volley of whistles and shouts of approval for a minute then slipped away.

"Gramp, you did it!" She ran to give him a hug. "You never told me Mountain Man was coming!"

"Good, he made it," Gramp said. "I wasn't sure. Any other surprises?"

"Yes, and you know about it, too, I bet!"

"We'll have a great fair, thanks to you, Mr. T." Sky predicted as she jogged to a stop beside them. "It was perfect! They rode in just as we were getting out of school. Everyone's going wild!"

"Mike's a born showman." Gramp grinned, shaking his head. "That man sure knows how to make a grand entrance. Let's go see if we can help them set up." Sky and Alex raced ahead of him.

"It's carnival time, ladies and gents! Step right up! Ten cents a try: show your brute strength and ring the bell!" Steven Tanner cried from the gaily decorated runway. He offered the heavy mallet to one of the ninth-grade boys. Flexing his muscles for the crowd, the young man hefted it high over his head and slammed it down on the weighted scale.

"Clang!" went the gong, triggering the red light on the tip of Paul Bunyan's nose.

"We have a winner!" Steve declared, handing a slithery plastic snake to the proud contestant. A line soon formed as his friends decided to show off their might.

"Peanuts, cotton candy, caramel apples! Come and get it!" Luis's mother proclaimed from a booth heavy with the wonderful aroma of buttered popcorn.

"Have you taken Tyler and Chandler to the petting zoo, Gramp?" Alex asked when she and her friends found him. A local farmer had set up the tiny zoo for families with younger children. He'd brought his baby llamas along with various breeds of rabbits, some goats, a litter of eight-week old kittens, plus five blackfaced sheep that rested in a grassy enclosure.

"Not yet," Gramp said. "They're waiting to ride the pony. We'll head there after we get a hot dog. Have you eaten, girls?"

"Yes." The four gave a vigorous nod.

"All health food, right?" Gramp grinned at them.

"Right!"

Nearby, a Shetland pony named Blondie made a youngster laugh as a volunteer led them around the temporary straw-covered corral.

"Come on, Gramp! Let's go! Blondie's ready," Chandler pulled on his hand, urging him toward the gate.

Mounted on the beautifully gentle pony, Chandler waved to his twin, who was content to sit inside the adjoining pen and cozy up to a furry, black-and-white, lop-eared rabbit until it was his turn to ride. Chan jiggled his boot heels against Blondie's belly, calling out, "Giddy-up!" The girls laughed when the Shetland paid no mind to her frustrated passenger and merely kept to a slow trot.

"The boys are use to riding with Dad and Gramp; their pace is a bit faster," said Alex.

They hurried off to play a hilarious chipmunk game. Each had a turn at the timed contest, eagerly pounding the plastic rodent as he popped out and just as quickly dropped back into one of many different burrows. Merry won a stuffed animal; the others chose colorful beaded bracelets. Moving on to the water-pond game, they flipped rubber frogs onto lily pads to win key chains and necklaces, adding them to their overloaded pockets.

"The hayride's next," shouted Sky, running to that popular booth for tickets.

Cheers rang out each time one of the two horse drawn wagons arrived or departed for the ten minute trek around the area. Sky and Merry, nestled deep in the thick hay along with some others, pitched handfuls of it all around. Alex and Paula happily perched on the thick yellow bales toward the back, clutching the wooden slats as they rolled along.

"Alex, come on, it's time to man the art booth," Sky reminded her as they drew to a stop. They jumped off the wagon, promising to introduce their friends to the Mountain Man later on.

"Sky, do me!" an impatient classmate begged from among the steady stream of fair-goers watching Skylyn put the finishing touches to a little boy's happy clown face.

"Cougar! Cougar!" Came the chant beside the booth as most of their junior-high friends eagerly paid to have their arms and faces decorated with the school logo—a snarling mountain lion.

"Your time's almost up, girls," their art teacher, Mrs. Berger said an hour later. "This was a super idea, Sky, and you both did fine! Thanks!"

Alexandra hurried to mix a new batch of brown paint to apply freckles to a youngster with bits of yellow straw still stuck in her hair. "There you are, Daisy Mae," she said. The smiling towhead rushed toward her parents. Alex stood to stretch just as another student slid into her chair, ready to put his artistic talents to work.

"Mountain Man Mike, I'm glad you and Jade made it to our fair and that you brought so many artifacts," Paula said, looking closely at the rare tomahawk-pipe he allowed them to examine in the tepee. He was careful to rewrap it in a skin and replace it in its rawhide box.

Jade went on to explain that the pipe and its colorful quilled box were very important to the Indians.

"They were treated with respect and used only for special ceremonial purposes because they were considered sacred."

"Sky and Alex have told us you can really throw a tomahawk." Merry smiled at Mike. "Will you show us?"

"Sure! I'll give you little ladies something to talk about, too," he said. He unhooked his favorite tomahawk from his belt, sauntered into the roped-off safety area, and took aim. The hawk flew true to course, whirling head over handle, to hit dead on target. The applauding audience called for more.

Jade Great Elk soon commanded their attention and made good on her promise. She whipped an arrow from her beaded quiver and proceeded to prove her ability with the bow and metal projectile. She stepped up, drew a bead on her target, pulled the string taut, and without a blink watched it rip through the center circle into the solid wall of protective hay-bales beyond.

"Phew!" came the collective sigh from her admirers.

"She nailed it! I don't think that'll ever come out," Sky said.

"I'm going to practice all summer," Luis said. "Just imagine doing that in archery club next fall—it'd be awesome."

"Okay, not to be outdone by my partner..." Mike said. Walking to his travois, he found a pigskin bag and reached inside.

"This, my young friends, is a true original!" he said as he pulled out a long-handled, double-bit ax. "Made with a solid hickory handle, this was a recognized American design favored by the settlers. It helped build our country!"

"Wow! I bet that could fell a few trees!" someone said.

"Right!" Mike said. "Not to mention build log cabins or make crude bridges and dugout canoes or rafts for river travel. As they moved west, early pioneers cleared the dense forests that covered the continent." He walked through the crowd, allowing each a chance to touch the two-headed ax.

"Can you toss this one, Mike?" Alexandra asked, rubbing the worn handle.

"Just watch!" he said with a twinkle in his eye. Moving several steps closer to a much thicker target, Mike heaved the double-bit straight at his mark. The crowd cheered.

"Tell us about the travois," Merry asked.

Jade drew her bay mare closer to her listeners.

"It's authentic Indian construction made with peeled lodgepoles and held together by strong hide straps." She unleashed the V-shaped carrier's bundle fastened to an elk-hide pelt that stretched between the two poles on each side of the horse.

"Cool! Can you sit on it? It'd make a neat carnival ride!" someone said.

"Sure." Jade nodded. "The Indians transported their children and their sick or elderly folks on them, but I think it must have been a bouncy ride."

"Trouble was you always knew where they were going," Sky spoke up. "And that could be either good or bad," she added, clearly catching their attention. "My grandmother told me the travois poles scratched telltale ruts in the dirt that made them easy to follow! For a long time the Indians didn't realize their enemies knew exactly what signs to look for," Sky finished in a solemn voice.

"They couldn't hide the marks by pulling them through a stream or over rocky ground, the way they did when traveling on foot," Mike reminded them. "But it was the only method of travel the ancients had before the Spanish brought horses to the Americas in the 1500s."

He went on to say that the dog travois was also an early mode of transport, enabling them to haul their small-size tepees. "Later, using horses made it possible to build and move much larger dwellings."

"The dogs were reluctant porters," Mike said with a chuckle. "They hated the job! And if they were unsupervised, they'd chase after jackrabbits or squirrels! It happened often, causing the small set-up of twig poles to bobble about, dumping their goods." His audience groaned at the frustrating thought.

"They hauled young children and their favorite dogs and puppies in a slightly safer, basket-like contraption," Jade added. "Indians loved their puppies, so they adopted the woven type of dog carrier because of possible attacks by wild animals that easily picked up dog scents."

"Sounds like a mini-Cinderella coach," Paula said, making everyone laugh.

Thanking Mike and Jade, the girls promised to look for them at the rodeo in September.

By nightfall the midway's glare drew more family fun-seekers anxious to try their luck at the games, most unaware they were keeping company with other nocturnal visitors. Above the strands of lights, a large orb-web spider looked around. Not fussy about where to trap its dinner cache of flies, assorted hard-shelled bugs, and mosquitoes, the eight-legged beauty set up shop on a string of red and blue flags. Beginning the lengthy task, its spinnerets, or silk glands, unraveled a wet, silky filament that quickly hardened into a sheer thread. Attaching it to a dim corner of the sno-cone booth, the spider stretched another dainty suspension bridge high in the air, latching it beside a red banner. Having completed its primary framework, the agile weaver was ready to spin the radial web with its sticky center.

A few hours later, an exhausted Alexandra plunked down her last quarter while waiting for her parents to clean up their stands. She ordered a grape shaved-ice treat, at the same time trying her best to dodge a hawkwinged moth on its way to buzz the irresistible lights above. Sky ambled up and ordered an orange ice. The large insect drew her attention as it bombarded the hot globe. Seeming to tire of the sport, it bobbed and dipped around the light one last time, darted off, and disappeared. Still curious, Sky followed it around the stand, only to walk headlong into the gummy bit of mesh belonging to the miniature predator.

"Euuww! Spiderweb!" Sky tried to pull away from the lacy filigree. She glanced up to discover a rainbow of iridescent colors whose surprised owner was backing away from the interfering outsider.

"Alex, help! The moth's caught, and so am I!"

Alexandra found her attempting to disentangle herself. She stepped close, took hold of Sky's sno-cone, and looked up. "Ah-h, there's that pesky moth." She inched closer to inspect. "It's history, now!"

"Hello! Am I here or not? Never mind the moth!" Sky complained.

"Just pull the stuff off!" Alex shot back.

"No! I don't want to break the web. She worked hard for it, and she needs her dinner!"

"Okay, Charlotte, send me a message, and I'll save you!" Alex returned the heated volley. Loving her own joke, she lifted her head, her whole body shaking with laughter. But knowing Sky's love of nature, she stood by and watched her friend work her way out, still trying to restrain her giggles.

"Don't worry," she couldn't help adding a few moments later, "spiders can repair their webs quickly and get right on with their sticky business!"

Free at last, Skylyn turned and pointed to the sno-cones.

"Okay, big helper! You were saying...?"

Alexandra glanced down to find herself clutching two squashed paper cups. Looking a bit farther, she noticed the icy blobs—one purple, the other orange—slowly coloring Sky's new white sneakers.

"Hey, sleepyhead, are you going to snooze all day?" Aggie said as she opened the blinds and sat down to ruffle the dark hair peeking out from the patches of sunlight highlighting Sky's quilt.

"Um-m-m, what time is it?" Sky mumbled. "Am I late?"

"It's ten-thirty, and you're done with school, remember? I have some news for you. Alex called, she wants you to bring Nambe over on Sunday night and spend a few days with her. And Raven's decided to come home and find a job around here for the summer."

"Oh, that's wonderful! Jeepers, I forgot it's vacation. Yippie!" Sky sat up and rubbed her eyes. "I'll go call Alex." She swung her legs over the side of the bed. "Wasn't the carnival great? I loved it. I wonder how much money we made? Maybe we can pay for the nursery plants now," Sky said, a frown beginning to crease her forehead.

"Don't worry; the PTA president promised to call when she gets the treasurer's tally," her mother said, lightly stroking Sky's back. They have to figure out the fair's expenses first, and the remainder will go to pay the bills for the overlook.

"I'm sure we did very well because the midway was packed all evening. Everyone was having a ball. Anne and I sold out of hot dogs and sodas twice, and we had to send for more."

"We ate our share of them," Sky admitted.

"Well, it's vegetables for you today!"

Official Detectives

"Boys, the second gate is as far as you're allowed to go, Alex reminded her brothers. "It's time to pedal your bikes back home. We'll see you later."

"Is it okay if we play here for a little while?" Chandler asked.

"All right, I'll give Mom a call and tell her where you are, Alex said, dialing her cell phone.

They hopped off of their small two-wheelers and went over to a rock pile under one of the globe willows lining the lane.

Goldie and Chester, wandered through the open gate, waiting while Alex reached down from her mount and closed it. They moseyed along, intending to cross the blacktop road and take the old wagon trail snaking through the forest. Glancing back a few minutes later Alex noticed the twins were nowhere in sight. She was satisfied they had headed home to pester Gramp or pursue other activities fit for active six-year-olds.

"There's Pie," Tyler said, his legs dangling from a low branch near Chandler. He pointed out the male black-billed magpie that had always trailed after them on family outings.

"He's so tame," Chandler said. "Maybe he'll come home with us again." He climbed down and crept slowly toward the sleek black-and-white bird. Perched on a boulder busily preening his lustrous tail, Pie stopped and cocked his head as if considering Chandler's idea. But unable to resist the lure of fresh animal tracks, he took off in a flurry and settled on the churned earth to search for a few roly-poly grubs.

When Ty saw his brother approaching the vine-covered fence, he called a warning about the barbed wire and not overstepping their boundary. But Chan stopped to watch the bird's explorations. He saw Pie's bill plunge into a hoofprint, his feet flicking up dirt as he hunted.

"Fly this way," Chandler begged.

"We have to go back," Tyler said.

"Wait here a minute. I'll try to get him to follow us the way he used to do," Chan said. He leaned his bike against the gate, climbed on the seat, and undid the latch.

"No! Mom will be mad! We better go home!" Tyler yelled. Chandler pushed his bike around the gate.

"Come back!" Ty tried again. Not wanting his brother to go alone, he started after him. They followed the busy magpie until he tired of the sport and flew away. They returned to the familiar rock pile that Gramp let them play on while waiting for Alexandra's school bus. Scrambling up, they settled into a position that gave them a clear view of the main road.

"Maybe if we wait for the postman and take the mail home for Mom she'll be less upset," Chandler said.

Sky and Alex pulled up beneath a fragrant awning of long-needled firs and slid off of their horses to rest on a fallen log. Thirsty, they took long draughts from their water bottles. Minutes later Chester and Goldie came crashing through the underbrush, their pink tongues lolling, both anxious for liquid refreshment.

"You've been chasing rabbits and anything else that moves and now you're all lathered like a race horse and dying for a drink. Okay!" Alex said, petting the doxie who sprawled on his back, feet in the air. Next to him sat Goldie, huffing and puffing.

"I'm sure Gramp packed extras." She rooted around in her saddle bag and found four more water bottles, plus two plastic dishes, and some homemade trail mix. She refilled the dogs' bowls twice before they were satisfied.

Jess drank thirstily from Alex's cupped hands, but her attention was elsewhere, her ears twirling. Alex followed Jess's gaze, now trained on a squirrel chattering at a young chipmunk that crossed its path. The chipmunk sat tall and held its ground at first, sizing up its challenger. Upon second thought, it gave way and dashed out of sight.

Lazing in the shadows, Nambe jingled his bit, enjoying the cold water that Sky trickled down his face.

"Look! He thinks it's bath time." Sky turned to find Alex peering into the treetops from which came a persistent chipping. A flash of red zipped across the ground as another squirrel paused, flicked its tail, and issued a stern warning. Sharp nails dug into the bark as it swung around the trunk and disappeared. The girls were glad to see it join its noisy neighbor, who was performing a high-wire act in the big top of overhanging branches.

"Do you think they mind the dogs?" Sky asked.

Alex chuckled at the sight of the exhausted pair snoozing in the dappled arbor, lost in their canine dream world.

"These sweethearts? Nah. Our ranch squirrels aren't even afraid of our barn cats." She turned back to wet Jess's face. Happy with the attention, Jess sidled closer, nudging her, hoping for more.

The girls reclaimed their seat in time to see the red squirrel scuttle off with something in its mouth.

"What's it carrying?"

"I couldn't tell—might be a pine cone. The female seems to be very protective. She might have a family," Alex whispered.

"I don't blame her—six big creatures have invaded her peaceful world."

"I guess," Sky agreed. "Maybe it'll help if we move." She roused the dogs, urging them across the clearing. "We'll have a good view from over there."

Quiet reigned once again in the little copse. The horses grazed nearby while the girls lay with their heads pillowed on their arms. They were happy to wile away the time on a cushion of fragrant needles, hoping for another glimpse of the squirrels.

"More wildlife to the right," Alex said when some chipmunk siblings caught her attention as they played under a couple of tumbled boulders,

"Big game!" Sky grinned.

The striking gray-and-white-layered rocks, probably deposited and compressed eons ago by the weight of a passing glacier, were now home-sweet-home to the miniature rodents. Three furry brothers hopped from rock to rock, scouting the neighborhood for food. It was a chore that soon turned into a jolly game of tail tag as each wee critter chased the other, never missing a beat in their rollicking twists and turns.

The girls howled with laughter, sending the chippies scrambling for cover.

"We're still too noisy," Sky said. "They probably won't dare appear until we leave—we're a menace to rodent society!"

"Wait a few more minutes. I want to see if they're adding to a storehouse somewhere. Gramp said he happened upon one years ago. It had thousands of pine cones and ears of corn piled high around the tree. He called it a squirrel *midden*, named after the ancient Indian mounds of discarded pottery shards and food. I'd love to find one."

"Sh-h-h!" Sky cautioned, clamping her hand over her mouth. "Squirrely's on the move." Once again they watched the little creature hurry away with something in its mouth. Back it came, repeating the journey a few minutes later.

"Now I know!" Alex caught her breath. "I saw a flash of bare skin; it's got a baby! Momma's moving the nest."

"Not because of us, I hope!" Sky worried.

"I don't think so. One was returning to the tree when we arrived—it must have been off constructing a new nest."

"That precious little baby was curled into a ball." Sky marveled. "It never moved a muscle as it bounced along in her mouth."

"That was so cool!" Alex said. "I wish my brothers could have seen it."

"I think I hear the mail truck coming, Chan," Tyler said, popping up to peer over a lavender sage bush growing in the crack of a boulder. "Let's hide." Loving the idea of a secret, Chandler agreed. They waited until the vehicle stopped, then peeked out at it. They saw a young man wearing jeans and a tight black T-shirt get out of the passenger's side of an old car whose noisy motor belched blue smoke. The man looked around, checking the area. Satisfied, he reached into the back and pulled out a small, light-colored bag with a strap on it. "Don't move, Ty," Chandler whispered.

Frozen, the boys watched as he whirled the thing above his head and let it fly. It sailed over the mailbox and disappeared into the thicket behind a wild blackberry patch. Hooting loudly, he jumped back into the car as the driver spun the tires. They sped away, leaving behind a rooster tail of dust.

"What were they doing?" Tyler asked his brother, who was still glued to the lichen-covered rocks. "Do you think they'll come back?"

"I don't know," he said. "But we'd better get out of here and go find Gramp." They scrambled down, snatched up their bikes, and headed for home.

"I wish the girls were with us," Ty said, pedaling as fast as his legs would go. Hurrying through the last gate, neither took the time to secure it. A few moments later they heard Gramp's Jeep in the distance. The way his 4x4 hared around the corner indicated his mood. When the sound of the engine slowed they knew he had spotted them.

"Uh-oh," was all a white-faced Tyler could say.

"Here comes trouble," Chan added. They swerved onto the grass and waited.

"Boys." Gramp dipped the brim of his black Stetson to shade his eyes. He peered at the tardy brothers. "We've been looking all over for you. Did you lose track of time as well as forget your mother's instructions?"

They shook their heads and began to talk at high speed. "There's something by the mailbox and..."

"Whoa! Hold it! No wonder we couldn't find you! You were way out of bounds, guys!"

"Yes, we know." Both admitted their guilt.

"But, but..." Chan sputtered, "some men did something funny, and we were hurrying home to tell you!" They talked; Gramp listened, nodding once in a while.

"You're not fooling me now, are you?" he asked, looking them directly in the eyes.

Minutes later with boys and bikes loaded up, they roared off to investigate. As soon as they stopped Ty slipped out of his seat belt. For once Chan followed his lead.

"Can you show me where the bag landed?" Gramp asked, opening his door.

No answer.

He swung around to find them lying flat on the floor. He shoved his hat to the back of his head.

"Okay, what's the matter?"

"Will they come back and get us?" Chan's muffled voice was barely audible with his face pressed tight in his folded arms.

"I don't want to get out," Ty whispered. Risking a glance, he peered up at his grandfather.

"I won't let them get you," Gramp promised. "Anyway, they're long gone by now!" He came to sit sideways on the seat above them.

"Let's play detective and try to find the bag. Then we'll be able to solve your mystery! Come on, I'll be right beside you."

Chandler raised himself up and pointed to a possible landing site. "It's over there." Gramp pulled him onto his lap. When Chan leaned down and tugged at his brother's arm, Ty scrambled up.

"Are my two officers ready to investigate the crime with me?" Gramp knew how to make them giggle. Chan slid off his lap and out of the Jeep. Tyler followed.

"This way, Captain." Tyler saluted and took his grandpop's hand to escort him to the scene.

An all-out search got underway as the three explored the area, trying to avoid the stickers on the blackberry canes.

"They hurt," griped Chandler, searching for a stick to lift the vines.

"Ouch," yelled Ty as another thorn found its mark. "Why didn't they throw it somewhere easy to find, like in the trees?"

Gramp stopped and rubbed his chin. "You know, you just might be on to something; it doesn't seem to be in here. Maybe we should look at the entrance to the old trail behind these sticky buggers!"

They cased their surroundings, one by one eliminating the ground under each tree and brush piles.

"Are you sure..." Gramp sighed, wiping the sweat from his brow.

"Yes!" they answered. Chan moved back to the brambles and continued poking around with his stick. Ty climbed onto a big stump for a better view.

"There it is, way high," he called. They followed the direction of his pointing finger, and there on a broken bough a white bag swung in the breeze.

"How are we gonna reach it, Gramp?" Ty asked.

"We go up." Tossing his hat on a bush, he grabbed a limb, and swung a leg over it.

"We're next! We get to climb, too!" Chan clapped, dancing around, ready to shinny up the tree.

"No! I mean I need you down there. Your job is to guide me to the right branch!" He glanced up, seeing only thick, green pine needles. "I still don't see it!"

"Go higher!" They sat Indian style on a log, intently watching his progress.

"What's happening over there!" came a shout that made the twins jump and swiftly drop to their knees behind Ty's stump, hearts pounding. Once again this very day it was Chandler who issued a command: "Stay down!"

"Tanner!"

"Yo!" Gramp's answer echoed over the hillside.
Failing to recognize his voice from on high, Ty and Chan grabbed each other, and shaking clear to the tips of their cowboy boots, held on for dear life.

"That you, Goddard?"

"Yeah!"

"Those men are back!" Ty whispered, trembling.

"No, I think it's someone else. Oh, I knew we should've paid better attention in Sunday school!"

"Where are you?" the stranger shouted.

"You'll never guess!" Gramp's now familiar voice answered. With a snap and crackle two booted feet landed next to them.

"Boys, where's your grandfather?" They glanced up at their new mailman. "You playing some sort of game with him?" They shook their heads.

"I'm in the tree, Jim. Don't scare them, please. Can you tell me exactly where the white pocket book is hanging up here?"

Hands on his hips, Jim looked up.

"Yep!" he said, "but, are you sure you got the matching shoes and gloves to go with that purse?"

"Sheriff? Robert Tanner here. I have a woman's shoulder bag that's probably been stolen. The name and address on the driver's license belong to a lady in Leadville." Gramp listened a moment. "No money in it, but several credit cards are there," he added. "A deputy's nearby? Great! We'll watch for him, thanks."

Chandler and Tyler each sat on an arm of Gramp's chair listening to every word.

"Boys, you did fine. The sheriff said he's proud of your detective work, and he wants to meet you!" Gramp said. "But you know he'll probably review the rules your parents set for you."

"They're for your well-being," their mother gently added.

"Hi, everybody!" The kitchen screen door slammed shut, punctuating the quiet. "We had a great ride, it was so peaceful!" Alex reached for the pitcher of iced tea, asking Sky to find two glasses. "Better than yours, I bet! You people probably sat around doing nothing all morning..."

A knock on the door jerked their attention to the figure on the other side. Alex walked over to see who it was.

"May I help you?"

"Do the Tanner twins live here?"

"Yes," she managed to say.

"Invite him in," Gramp said, urging the boys off of his chair. Alex opened the door, and Steven went over to greet him.

"Dave, glad to see you," he said, shaking hands. He introduced the rest of the family and gave him the purse. "The boys are right here." Gramp propelled them forward, introducing them with a proud smile.

"I'm Deputy Dave," he said, crouching down to their level. "I'm glad to meet you two heroes! Thanks for being so alert. I'm sure the lady will be glad to have her wallet and important papers back. She was very worried about them. Now I have something for you." Alex and Skylyn looked on.

"Did the men hurt her?" Chandler asked after the officer had pinned a gold deputy's star on his shirt.

"No, thank goodness. They grabbed it out of her shopping cart in the supermarket parking lot and ran."

"I'm glad she's okay," Tyler said. He examined Chandler's award and his own shiny new badge. Reaching out to touch Dave's star, he beamed at the deputy. "Now all three of us are twins!" Steven turned to the girls with a wide grin.

"A boring morning, huh?"

Summer Stars

"What kind of job is Raven looking for, Mom?" Skylyn asked as they lingered over a quiet Saturday morning breakfast.

"Something part-time, and I don't blame her." Aggie said. "She's burned out from studying for two solid years without a break. And right now she needs a few good days of rest."

"I'm glad she's home; it seems like old times." Sky got up to rinse her plate and stack it in the dishwasher. She took a moment to bathe in the glorious stream of sunlight flowing through the large window over the sink. She caught sight of Strudel, curled up tight, snoozing away on the old sodbarrow.

"I think I'll go out to the barn and see if I can help Dad and John." She started away then paused. "I hope Raven has time to give Apple Pie some attention. Rave's always been so good with her, and that sweet Appaloosa's crazy about Raven."

"I know, and you're great with Apple, too, honey. I wish I had more time to ride, but Dad and Taggart try to get her out for a run as much as possible when they're home," she said. "Someday you'll discover that when kids go away to college, parents are left in charge of their pets."

Strudel stretched his paws out when Sky gently wakened him. She dropped down beside him, gave his sleep-warmed body a hug, and pulled him onto her lap. She nestled her forehead into his wiry curls. "Pupski, you better be prepared to study your ABCs." Gently holding both of his floppy ears, she looked deep into his dark eyes. "Because when I go off to college, you're going with me!" The little white dog gave her nose a sloppy swipe of his tongue. Wise beyond his doggie years, Strudel snuggled a bit closer for more loving attention.

"Any luck, honey?" Aggie asked, slicing a thick roast beef sandwich in half. She handed it to her eldest daughter and poured two tall glasses of lemonade.

"Nothing promising," Raven said. "Everybody wants full-time workers." She sat down at the table to chat with her mother. "I saw Pam Rogers in town. She wants me to help her if I have any spare time. I'd love to do it, but it's all volunteer."

"I remember. You couldn't wait to turn sixteen so you could take Apple with you," Aggie said. "You really liked working with those kids, and Dad enjoyed his time there, too."

"It was very rewarding, and I loved it; but I also want to earn some money for college. I mind spending yours all the time."

"Well, don't worry; something will come along soon. Talk to Pam again. Maybe you'll have time to help her until you get a job."

"I just might do that," Raven said, brightening. "I don't want to sit around doing nothing. Maybe she could fit me in a few early morning slots. I'll work any part-time job around those hours," she said, happy to have made a firm decision. Her mother agreed.

"Ask your sister if she'd like to go along and help. It would keep her occupied for the summer. Maybe Alex's parents will let her volunteer, too!"

"Good idea. It's too bad they're not old enough to help with the riders. They'd be great around the stables, though."

"I can go with you? Oh, Rave! I'd love it!" Sky cried. "This is fabulous! I used to cry when you two drove away with Apple and Eagle in the old horse trailer. Nan kept explaining that it was your special thing to do with Dad, and someday it would be my turn."

"I'm glad you're going with me," Raven said. "But I start at 7:30 a.m. three days a week. We'll have to load Apple in the van and be on the road before 6:15."

"I'll help! I love doing that stuff, and Appy's an easy loader," Sky said. "Rave, I can see why your friend wants you and Apple back; you're both gentle with kids."

"Thanks, sis, but there's even more. Mom called Alexandra and asked if she'd like to meet us there. She's over the moon about it, too." Sky took her sister's hands and danced her all around the kitchen.

"Horses for the Handicapped." Sky read the sign as they turned in to Hopewell Farms early Monday morning. "This will be a great summer! I want to meet the kids."

"You will, but remember, they aren't all children. Pam's working with a sixty-four-year-old gentleman who's had a stroke. He's trying to get his strength back, and he's had to learn to walk and talk and ride all over again."

"Wow! That must be hard to take, especially if you love horses." Sky shook her head. "Gee whiz, I've known how to ride since I was three. I can't imagine forgetting how to do it!"

"There's Alex." Raven spotted her standing with Gramp beside his Jeep, surrounded by a host of cats and three ranch dogs who gave them a wagging hello.

"Welcome," Pam greeted them. "It's a banner day: four new volunteers! I'm so grateful!" Pam said. "I remember Raven when she was a teenager. She and Joseph were a great help, as I know Sky and Alex will be. Our fourth person is Alex's grandfather."

I didn't know! That's wonderful, Gramp!" she said, holding two thumbs up.

"He says since he has to bring you, he'd like to work with us," the petite blonde said. "And he's a farrier, too! Right now I've got two barefoot dapple grays crying out for brand new shoes."

Continuing their orientation, Pam gave them a tour of the stables, corrals, and two large barns housing the eight horses belonging to the national organization. A cool breeze flowed from several circulating fans as well as through the east-west openings in one of the barns. Each stall had windows with wooden shutters that could be closed at a moment's notice in case of bad weather. Three equine residents poked their heads outside to enjoy the shade from an overhanging tree and watch the activity in the corral.

Alex and Sky noted the huge wooden trusses housing at least three barn swallow nests.

"There's a familiar sight," Sky said, pointing out a slender, bluish-black bird serving lunch to its noisy youngsters. Its arrival on the plastered-mud nest triggered a hungry response from the babies, who popped up, like three jacks-in-a-box. "Tchee-tchee," they begged with their mouths wide open, making their yellow-lined throats an easy target for the deposit of a plump bug or juicy berry.

"Our favorite colonists," Gramp said, watching yet another of the sociable swallows dive through an open window with its beak full. "That one's probably been following the farmer's tractor for grasshoppers that are trying to escape!" It swooped up to light on the side of a rustic beam, its sharp nails and forked tail feathers easily holding it steady.

"We have a resident barn owl, too." Pam said. "You'll have to look closely to find her, though."

They searched the upper reaches of the structure and finally located the slender owl with its unique, heart-shaped face. Resting comfortably with one leg drawn into her downy white breast, she soon became aware that she was the center of attention. Bobbing her head forward for a better view, and tilting it from side to side as if sizing up the rude intruders, she blinked her wide dark eyes.

"They usually choose hollow trees or abandoned buildings, but she doesn't seem to mind our company because she comes back each year to raise her family," Pam said. "If we get too noisy she'll hiss once in awhile."

"She's reminding us she's nocturnal, and it's her sleep time," Gramp said.

At home in any barn, he remained behind to check on the tools available for shoeing the horses.

Sky and Alex were happy to meet the teens cleaning stalls, spreading the mixture of sand and fresh sawdust, and filling the hayracks. They were impressed with the cleanliness of the horses' quarters. Sky found a brush to scrub one of the water buckets. Alex uncoiled a hose to rinse and refill it.

"That's the kind of volunteers you fall in love with!" Pam beamed her approval.

"What comes next?" Sky asked.

"I always have a mile-long list, mostly housekeeping chores like Tommy, Jenny, and Shane are doing," Pam said. "After that look for anything you think needs attention, the way you just did. It's called initiative—you automatically used plain old horse sense!"

"Would you like to work in the tack room?" she asked as they strolled over the antique brick paving running between the rows of stalls. The girls nodded.

"Then that's a good place to start; it needs rearranging. When we finish the tour, I'll get you settled in over there."

"Like Raven, some of our helpers bring their own horses. We screen them carefully to make sure they're gentle enough for our particular riders," she said. "All must have good dispositions. They can't get spooked around strangers, especially those whose handicaps require wheelchairs, walkers, canes, crutches, or braces."

"Mild-mannered horses like Apple," Raven spoke up, "are perfect around children wanting to pat, poke, and hug them or even pull their tails!"

"That's right," Pam said. "But some people have disabilities that aren't evident." She spoke of those people in the early stages of muscular diseases, those suffering from fears of some sort, or children who have stopped speaking for reasons known only to themselves—maybe from being abused or battered.

Raven went off to talk with Pam's assistant and to meet the children she'd be working with while Pam and the girls made their way to the tack room.

"Clean up; do whatever it takes to keep the leathers in good condition. The saddle soap is on the shelf." She pointed it out. "All the rigs need a hefty dose of tender loving care, just like the people who come to ride. What doesn't get done today we'll work on next time! Have fun!"

Standing on a three-legged stool, Alex began pulling harnesses off of their pegs. Next she tackled the shelves, dumping their contents in heaps on the floor and wiping away cobwebs that hadn't seen the light of day in a century.

Laughing in between sneezes, Alex located dust cloths and cans of polish and set to work. The aged knotty-pine woodwork soon took on a soft, golden glow.

Sky lugged piles of the colorful, woven horse blankets outside and gave each a good shaking.

She dropped one on a patch of grass and sat down on it to have a moment of rest. Separating the older woolen squares from the newer, Sky folded each in half and soon found herself sharing her soft seat with a white barn kitten. Used to visitors, it promptly snuggled next to her, gently pawing at her hands as she worked.

"The walls and shelves look great!" Sky complimented Alex an hour later. "And the blankets are aired and ready to go back," she said. Sky handed her a neatly folded pile with the white kitty perched on top.

"Ah," Alex said. "Lucky girl, you've had company while you worked. All I had were spiders and an empty mouse house!" She poked her finger into the tiny opening by a knot in the paneling. "It's no wonder the kitten wanted to play—the mice are away!"

When Alex hopped down and pushed the stool aside, Sky seized the broom, anxious to sweep the wide plank floor and finish the job.

"I'm happy about the harnesses; they really needed attention."
Alex backed out of her partner's way. "Next time we'll do the
saddles."

"Okay, but right now let's get some cold water from the ice
chest and head for the corral," Sky said. "Pam wants us to watch
the riding before we leave."

Waiting in a shady spot under a cottonwood tree, Raven was
grateful for the drink her sister brought her. She was ready for
her last rider, a beautiful eight-year-old blonde named Jill with
heavy casts on both legs.

"What happened to her?" Sky whispered.

"She was in a car accident, sitting in front next to her mother.
Her legs were badly broken."

Horrified, Alex asked if she had been wearing a seatbelt.

"Yes," Rave said, "but they were hit on the passenger side."

"How much longer does she have to wear them?" Sky asked.

"She's mending fine and only has a few months to go. She
loves horses, and she begged her doctor to sign the papers for her
to ride. I'll be her leader with Nancy and Laurie as her side walkers. Watch us!" Raven said. Handing her bottle to Sky, she led
Apple over to the mounting platform.

Jill's mother waited with her, and Pam came up to greet them.

"Ready to ride, little gal?" she asked, ruffling Jill's hair. She
settled a safety helmet on her head. "Come on, let's go see Apple
Pie and Raven!" Jill waved her on, impatient to start. Pam pushed
the youngster's wheelchair up the ramp to the platform, where
she, Raven, and the others lifted her out and settled her in the
saddle. Raven cinched the belt tight and helped her get comfortable, joking about having warm Apple Pie without ice cream.
Raven allowed her time to get used to the animal, who stood
quietly through it all.

"I love your pink casts, honey, but I think they need some seri-

ous decorating!" Raven said. "When we're through, Apple and I will sign them for you! What do you think of that?"

"I think Apple Pie will have to do it very carefully!"

"Let's go, Apple," Jill urged, clutching the saddle horn. Holding the lead rope, Raven nodded to the two girls in place on either side. Each held a leather strap hooked to the wide belt around Jill's middle. They started circling the corral.

Glad to throw her cares to the wind, Jill's face brightened. She gave a happy shout when Raven started to jog, encouraging Apple to go a bit faster, giving her something to remember for her first time back in the saddle.

Sky and Alexandra listened, soaking up the action, pledging to help the disabled when they turned sixteen in two years. It was exciting to think Jessie and Nambe might play a part in the therapy as well. Just being here to help in any capacity was enough for now.

"I can't wait till Wednesday," Sky said as she rechecked the halter leads and put a good portion of hay in Apple's rack. "Here's your reward for a good deed, Appy." Patting the horse's rump, she jumped out of the van when Raven called for her.

Sky adjusted her seat belt a fraction tighter and relaxed as Raven swung around and headed down the drive.

"I was proud to hear you two did a terrific job in the tack room. You can see that Pam really needs the help."

"It was lots of fun," Sky said. "You were wonderful with your charges, Sis. Seems like you were born for that job." Sky couldn't help beaming at her.

"Want to stop at McDonald's for a burger and fries?"

"You have to ask?" Sky said. "By the way, if you're going through the drive-in, give Appy a chance at the window—she'll be wanting something more filling than hay."

"It was so neat." Sky greeted her mother when she came home from work. "Rave did a great job. I loved meeting the volunteers," she chattered on nonstop. "Most are teens, and Alex and I hope we can get to know them better. We watched them clean the stalls..."

"Gramp, I'm glad you stayed to help," Alex said. "I'm trying to think of what other things we could do beside cleaning, though." "Those chores are just as important as what the leaders and side-walkers do, honey," he said.

"Oh, I know that, but there must be something we could do to brighten the time they have to spend waiting for their rides home. It should be something Sky and I can get directly involved in, but I just can't seem to think of what it might be," Alex said.

"Knowing you two, I'm sure you'll come up with something. Shall we have lunch at the Farmer's Market? I want to get some string beans for dinner. You know how much I like them with ham and potatoes."

They pulled into the town square and walked around the outdoor market that had been there since he was a kid. Alex got her hot dog, and Gramp chose a sausage sandwich loaded with peppers and onions.

"Let's find us a mess of beans and head on out," he said after they'd eaten.

Alex loved to visit the old-time market held three days a week from spring until fall. Attending was almost a ritual for farmers selling their wares and getting together with old friends.

"Early each Monday, Thursday, and Saturday farmers used to pull into town in mule carts or horse-drawn wagons filled with produce from gardens and orchards," Gramp told her as they waited for the woman to weigh his purchase.

"They fashioned display tables out of old boards laid across barrels set under the trees or topped with a cloth sunshade staked in the ground. Sometimes people just sold their goods directly from their wagons. They were as happy as new mother hens to share news or exchange recipes."

They made simple booths out of crates to show off their woven baskets brimming with vegetables, eggs, and cut flowers that added color to the stall. Home-canned jellies and jams, plus a delicious offering of baked goods made it even more tempting to the shoppers. Farmers and their wives sat right in the middle of it all.

"I can still taste the spicy pumpkin and sweet-potato pies, not to mention the gingerbread!" Gramp said, smacking his lips.

"Better watch out for your stomach, Gramp. I think you're on a food kick!"

"Except for the wood crafts and the fast-food stands, the market still has the flavor of the old-time gathering that my family visited at least once a week," Gramp said, easing his way back into traffic.

"Let's come again and spend more time looking around," Alex said. "You know how I like old things—especially that hot-dog stand with the antique microwave!"

"My mother sewed her own clothing," Gramp said, ignoring her remark. "During the long winters she made beautiful quilts with leftover cloth. She made aprons from the scraps and sent them to town for her friend, Emily, to sell."

"She was smart to earn her own spending money," Alex said. "I think she'd fit in very well today."

"She sure would!" Gramp enjoyed the thought. "They called it 'pin money' because the women used it to buy their pins and other sewing needs. You have one of her quilts on your bed, but I have others packed away in her old cedar chest. Remind me to get them out for you to see."

"I know that quilt patterns have names," Alex said. "I'd like to learn to recognize some of them. Mom told me mine's called Star of Bethlehem and also Texas Star. Some might have two or even three names. I especially love the red, white, and blue in the giant star. I plan to keep it forever," Alex said.

"I had a star quilt, too. That cotton coverlet was so comfortable and cool, it was my favorite. Long before my brothers were born I had a wonderful golden retriever named Candy. One September day she got sick, and I didn't want to go to school and leave her," Gramp said. "Mother and Dad promised they would take the dog to the veterinarian. Reassured, I went off to school.

"Mother told me that she held Candy on her lap on the way to town. Just before they reached the vet's office, Candy looked up at her, gave a sigh, and died quietly in her arms. They waited for me to come home to choose her burial spot. With tears flooding my eyes, I ran upstairs to my room. When I returned, I helped bury her beneath her favorite weeping willow, wrapped in my star quilt."

"What did your mother say?"

"She knew that was exactly what I'd do." He gave a wisp of a smile as memories surged through him. "Candy was so special. Nothing could have been more fitting for such a perfect companion."

"I think Candy was your very own special star," Alex said, reaching out to take his hand. "Did you ever have another quilt?"

"It was sitting under the Christmas tree that December. I found out later my mother worked on it every evening after I went to bed to finish it in time."

"What was the design?" He merely smiled at her.

"Wait a minute!—was it the star quilt that I have?" Gramp nodded.

"I never knew, and thanks for telling me about part of your youth. I'll remember it always because I want to keep our family traditions alive. Mom says quilts are a big part of today's world—and they're very collectible. Some record historic events—almost like Indian rock carvings and picture tepees! I'm so glad about the way Great-grandmother Tanner kept herself occupied during the long winter!"

"That she did, lassie! She also knitted our mittens, caps, and scarves," he said. "I used to sit beside her and watch her work. I can still hear the sounds of her needles clicking away! I never figured out how she could talk and knit at the same time! Boy, we wore those woollies to shreds from sledding, skiing, or just doing our chores. We kept her busy year round at that task, but if she ever had any extras, she'd pack them off to market with

Emily."

In many small towns across America, farmers and crafters in their pick-up trucks and vans still follow the same marketing tradition, converging on the central square, now probably paved over and equipped with traffic signals.

Celebrities

"I've got it, Gramp!" Alex yelled from the top of the stairs. Receiving no answer and knowing no one else was home, she hopped on the well-worn banister and slid down to find him snoozing through his favorite TV western. She knelt beside his chair, jiggled his arm, and softly called his name.

"Huh?" he sputtered.

"I have the idea!" she repeated. He shook his head to clear it. "You know," she insisted, "the one I was searching for on our ride home yesterday."

"I give up," he mumbled, slumping down for more shut-eye. "Gramp, stay awake. I need to run this by you," she chided.

"Okay," he sighed, sitting up. "Go ahead, it's past my bedtime, but I'm sure you'll tell me anyhow. Let me get a cup of coffee."

"It's only nine-thirty. Stay put; I'll make it." He gave her his full attention when she returned. Drawing the ottoman close, she sat down and leaned toward him...

"Not bad," he said a few minutes later, taking another sip of

177

the strong, hot brew. "Not bad at all."

"What!" She bristled, sitting back with her hands on her hips. "My idea or the coffee?" Wide awake now, he set his cup down.

"Wait'll Pam hears about it," he said, looking at the almost empty cup. Alex jumped up.

"I suppose I won't get any more out of you till it's been re-filled!" She hustled to the kitchen. "Well, now you'll be awake until the cows come home!" He gave a hoot of laughter. This time she had added a plate piled high with chocolate cookies to the tray.

Hurry up, Rave!" Sky called from the bottom of the stairs. "I want to see Alex; we've got places to go, people to see, and things to do!"

"I'm coming, but it's early yet for heaven's sake!" And she thought she'd have trouble rousting her out of bed. Raven passed her father on the stairs. "Sky's just like you, Dad—up early and out!"

"Right! We've got Appy loaded and raring to go!"

"So's ole what's-her-name, apparently!" Raven groused, mimicking Sky, "I've got places to go, and blah, blah, blah..."

"Good morning, Sunshine," Sky said. "May I get you iced tea or coffee with your bagel and cream cheese?"

"Tea would be nice, thanks."

"Lemon with that?"

Raven sat down and leveled a sleepy eye on her. "Why are you waiting on me?"

"I'm happy to do it for such a nice sister," Sky replied.

"I'm afraid to think what the consequences might be."

"Not to worry! It's all good. We've got plans for Hopewell Farms that will blow your mind!"

"Tell me," Raven urged, sipping her tea, feeling more awake.

"Wait and see!" Sky set a warm bagel on a napkin in front of her.

"Come on." She bit into the toasty treat and followed it with a sip of tea. "Give! Or else we don't leave the driveway."

"All right, I promise you'll get the whole story on the way—so let's go. Sky snatched her sister's purse and keys, dangled them at her, and dashed out of the house. "I'll start the engine for you!"

"No, you won't! Don't even think about moving that truck! Remember Apple Pie's in there!" Rave scooped up her bagel and chased after her. "Geeze! Next she'll be hounding me for driving lessons!"

"Hi, Alex!" Sky called from her perch on the corral fence. "Morning Mr. T. How are you?"

"Don't ask him, Sky. He's gretzy this morning. His stomach is giving him fits."

"Humph! It's the late night food you forced on me."

"You okay, Robert?" Pam asked when she joined them. "Maybe you should have stayed home today."

"Nah! Anne said the same thing, but I'll be fine once I get going." He shook off her concern.

"Good job, girls! The saddles gleam like silk. They haven't looked this good in years. And Alex" Pam added, "I love your idea. It will give you some time with the riders. You've met Janine, our newsletter editor. Get together with her before you leave. Sky, you have my permission to start on Friday. It could become a regular end-of-the-week activity. The nicest part of it is that you can work together on both projects. Way to go!" Pam slapped high-fives with them, and off she went.

"Yes! It's Friday!" Alex said to her mom and sleepy little Chester. She hopped off the bottom stair and leaned down to pet the dachshund. "Janine says I'll have my own by-line!" She went to search the kitchen cupboard for a bowl.

"Sounds wonderful; I'm very proud of you," Anne said as she stirred sugar into her mug. She watched Alex add fresh blueberries to her Cheerios and top it off with banana slices. Adding a good measure of skim milk, she dug her spoon deep into her creation.

"Slow down so you can digest it properly, please," Anne cautioned as she slid onto the banquette, automatically leaving space for Chester, who was already begging to get up.

"Oh, my gosh." Alex leaned back and took a deep breath. " What if I mess up and can't do it?"

"Honey, calm down. If you'd take your time and try not to inhale the cereal, your brain would work better."

"Be serious, Mom! I've done my research on interviewing people, and I made a list of questions, but what if I pick someone who can't talk!"

"Negativism won't get you anywhere," Anne said. "I know you can think for yourself. After all, you came up with the whole concept! Remember your dad's famous law: There are no rules chiseled in stone. You just solve those puppies right on the spot."

"Whatever that means," Alex said, pushing her bowl away.

"It's called being able to think on your feet." Anne took a sip of her coffee. "Now that I think about it, I must say you're right about one thing: it will be a challenge, like those thousand-piece jigsaw puzzles you and Gramp work on." Anne spread fresh apple butter on her toast. "Would you avoid Jill if she had that type of problem instead of broken legs?"

"No, I'd try to find another way to communicate with her."

"Okay, what would you do?"

Alexandra thought for a minute.

"I'd ask questions she could answer by nodding or shaking her head."

"Body language—that's a good start."

"I guess it is." Brightening a bit, Alex sat up.

"See? You'll do fine. You came up with a working plan just like that!" Anne snapped her fingers. "Now, finish that mountain of cereal and we'll get going."

"You're driving? What's the matter with Gramp? Is he sick?"

"He's okay, but his stomach's still bothering him, so he decided to sleep in this morning."

"I want to see him," Alex insisted.

"Let him rest; he'll be fine. He has the medicine Dr.Cash prescribed for him last week."

"When did he see him? I didn't know about that. Now I am worried, Mom, and I don't want to go to Hopewell. I never should have given him those cookies the other night." She banged a fist on the table.

"Dad's off today, so he'll be around to keep an eye on him."

"I peeked in. He was snoring up a storm, but I still don't feel right about leaving," Alex said later as they started off.

"I've got the cellular phone; we can come home immediately if needed. Now relax and stop fretting."

While waiting for Sky and her sister, Alex introduced Anne to Jill and her mother. The girls showed them the newly installed fish pond with a miniature wishing well on the front lawn of the Hopewell farmhouse.

"Lots of wishes have been made already," Jill said. "It's loaded with coins." Rolling her chair closer to toss in six brand new pennies, she turned and smiled up at Alex. "I bet you know what I'm wishing for."

"And it won't be long till it comes true." Alex whipped a packet of colored pens from her pocket and knelt down.

"I didn't forget my promise."

"Mom, let's see what she wrote." The eight-year-old waved her mother closer and leaned over to read the message on her left cast. "Dear Jill, You're a star—hope all your wishes make you well. Love, Alex." Blue stars surrounded the message. Six brown pennies in a wishing well decorated the other.

"I love it," she said. "Thanks Alex."

"Open for business!" Sky announced. She put a rickety snack table on the sidewalk by the small pool and set out her paints and brushes. Tearing the wrap off a roll of paper towels, she settled down on the three-legged stool she'd rustled from the tack room.

"C'mon, Mr. Yeager! How about being my first customer of the day?" she called to a man she had met earlier.

"Okay, young lady, I'm game," he answered. He took his time walking, steadying himself with a four-pronged cane. Sky held her breath, ready to assist him if necessary. She remembered Pam's instructions that he needed to make his way on his own to gain confidence and preserve his dignity. At last he made it to the lawn chair next to Sky.

"I'd like to be a clown."

"A clown it is!" she answered, and set to work. She never noticed the small group that quietly gathered—a few women in wheelchairs, two girls on crutches, and a boy in his dad's arms, fresh from his horseback ride. Sky daubed on a final bit of rouge and held up a mirror for him.

"You're looking good!" She patted his shoulder. If we had a black hat, you could be the famous Emmitt Kelly." She whirled around at the sound of cheers. "Looks like business is picking up!"

"I want big red lips like that," the youngster told her.

Alexandra was very busy with pen and paper. She worked the crowd, talking to each guest and scribbling away on her pad. She stopped at Sky's table to take hold of Mr. Yeager's arm and guide him to the pool's stone surround.

"I'm Alexandra Tanner. I think you make a handsome clown." May I interview you for our newsletter? We could sit here where it's nice and cool." He nodded and carefully formed his words.

"I'd like that, Alexandra," he said. Letting go of his cane, he extended his hand for her to shake. Shifting sideways, he turned his palm up to catch a hint of the mist rising from the fountain.

"Feels good," he said, with a wobbly grin. They sat in silence, watching a bold Steller's jay land nearby. He stole a quick sip, gave an impertinent flick of his steel-blue topknot, and took off with a raucous squawk.

"He likes the cool water, too," Mr. Yeager said.

"Ask your mom if you can come over for the weekend," Sky suggested that afternoon. Alex set off to find Anne.

"She'll bring me over later," Alex reported. "Right now I want to go home to see how Gramp's doing."

"Did you get to meet Mr. Yeager?" Alex asked her mother as they drove away. Anne nodded.

"Before or after Sky got finished with him?"

"Before. He's a very nice man. Pam says he's working hard on his exercises. I think he's got the strength of mind and the right attitude to conquer his disability."

"I was with him afterwards, and I really enjoyed it," Alex said. "He was lots of fun. We talked mostly about his childhood. I wondered, but of course it was impolite to ask why he had to use the cane. Is the weakness in his left arm and leg from a stroke?"

"Yes, it usually leaves one side or the other with some paralysis."

"What happens when someone has a stroke?"

"Well," Anne hesitated, taking a quick glance at her daughter. A blood clot lodges in a vein or an artery, blocking the blood supply to the brain. It's like unplugging the power to a computer. A blockage in the brain sort of does the same—it turns off a part of the body.

"Can a person get over it?"

"Some do. I've read there are new drugs that work well if they get the victim to a hospital right away. Later on therapy will help the paralysis if the person has a positive outlook and the determination to work at it. Some lose their will and just give up."

"My family better stay positive," Alex said.

"Dawn patrol!" Joseph woke the girls early Saturday morning. Plying him with questions produced only a promise of being in for something special. They piled into the truck after breakfast and headed east to greet the sun. Sky and Alex played a guessing game about their destination. As soon as they turned north toward the hills, they knew the answer.

"You'll be surprised at the changes," Joe said as they rounded a bend, affording them their first glimpse of the overlook at Buffalo Meadows. He pulled up to one of the wooden car stops Tag had made.

"Look at the wildflowers Pat planted. Her seeds have turned the bare dirt into a garden of Eden—she'll love it!" Alex said, skipping down the winding path, cheering each plant and shrub as she passed.

"We'll have to call her," Sky said. Her father laughed.

"Don't bother, kiddo. She phoned us to make sure we'd get her favorite girls over here."

"We should have known she'd be visiting her babies."

Joseph was proud of the flourishing embankment Rob and Raven had created. Signaling for silence, he pointed to the red spikelet on the star-shaped century plant. It was providing breakfast for a black-chinned hummingbird. Unconcerned by certain guests, the hummer wasn't about to tolerate others; it chased off an opalescent-winged dragonfly clutching a stem on needle-like legs. Streaking back, the bird reclaimed its territory and hovered in front of a crimson, trumpet-shaped flower. Probing its Lilliputian beak deep inside, it uncurled its tongue and licked up the honey-sweet nectar.

Flitting from blossom to blossom on the tall cluster, it sipped to its heart's content, unknowingly making Mother Nature smile at its tiny face liberally dusted with golden pollen.

"It must be a female—it's wearing powder!" Sky whispered as they watched the bird at work.

"Go for it, girl!" Alex said, "Spread your flower power among our plants!"

Later, seated on a picnic bench under a colorful Dairy Queen umbrella, Joseph ordered frozen yogurt for them. He turned to Alex.

"I bet your grandfather will be anxious to see it when he hears about the pass."

"If ever he gets to feeling better," she said.

"Pam will love this, Al." Skylyn had a chance to preview Alex's new "Spotlight" column as they lounged on beanbag chairs in her bedroom. "You've got the description of Mr. Yeager's cosmetic do down pat! Jeepers, it was such fun. I can't wait for our next face-painting Friday."

"Lucky you. I'll have to wait a whole month to see my column in print," Alex said. "I just had a thought—the article would look super with an illustration. I wish you'd take your drawing pad on Monday and sketch some of the people on their horses."

"Fantastic idea!" Sky clapped her hands. "Why didn't I think of it?" She scrambled up to search through her desk drawers. "I'm into it now," she said, holding a charcoal stub aloft and drafting Alex as her first subject.

"I packed a few snacks to tide you over," Aggie said to Sky and Alex when she dropped them off Monday morning. "Anne and I will meet in town and go shopping. We'll have an early lunch and be back around one o'clock."

The girls checked the riding list. They would first work with the horses then go to meet the two riders suffering from multiple sclerosis.

"The ladies are due at eleven o'clock. I hear they're crazy about their horses, and I hope they'll let me sketch them in action," Sky said. "Right now, I'm itching to get my hands on Sweetie, that beautiful palomino. I'm to curry and brush her and a few of the others, too."

"I'll be in the shower stall with Teddy Bear, the pony. He loves water, so we'll have fun." They chattered as they collected supplies for their jobs.

"Al, come see Sweetie!" Sky climbed the side of Teddy's stall to watch her rub him dry. She wrung out the wet chamois and hung it on a post before following Sky to where the mare stood, poking her nose over of the bottom half of the dutch door.

"Ta-da!" Sky sang, waving her hand.

"She looks devine!" Alex said, admiring the blond mane done in a perfect french braid along the crest of her neck.

"Ahem!" Sky cleared her throat. "You might want to check the reverse side as well." Alex stepped through the gate, stroking Sweetie's velvet skin as she walked by. She saw Sky had given equal attention to the tail, replete with a rose-colored bow.

Their giggles, made the horse, now tired of silly girl-stuff, give a snap of her stylish tail.

"It's a swatter with horsepower!" Sky said, rubbing her stinging cheek. "Let's get out of here while we can!"

"Girls, I'd like you to meet Dianne and Mandy," said Faye, Pam's assistant. The youthful-looking grandmothers sat patiently in their car waiting for Brian to help them get out.

"Skylyn is great with charcoal and pencil, and she would like to sketch you. Maybe you'll see yourselves in our monthly newsletter," Faye said.

"Sounds like fun," they agreed.

"Here's our strongman now!" Dianne said, waving.

"Dianne's up first, riding Cody. Max will soon be ready for Mandy," Brian said. He retrieved a wheeled walker from the rear car seat and quickly unfolded it. Mandy slid her legs sideways and held her arms out to him.

"Point me over there, please," she said, indicating the girls' locker room.

"I've brushed down Cody," Sky said, moving to the driver's side to talk to Dianne. "He's so calm, I can see why you like him. I want to draw him in color someday."

"He's my favorite. I can't wait to get here. When I'm on him, it gives me a feeling of freedom," the lively, dark-haired woman said. "I can't depend on my legs anymore, but when I'm riding I have a sense of control again."

"Off you go: Max will wait for you," Brian said to Mandy, watching her carefully. She pushed her walker onto the grass and slowly made her way to the building, one tiny step at a time.

"Dianne's next!" Brian said. "Are you ready, young lady?" .

"Ready as I'll ever be. I've been a rider all my life, but today my legs are sending me another message. I think you'll have to carry me." She fastened the snap on her safety helmet and met him with outstretched arms. He gently scooped her out of the car and headed for the mounting platform. He carried her straight up the steep ramp and gently set her on her feet. With a heartfelt sigh and her helper right beside her, Dianne steadied herself, grasped the rails and waited. "I'm right where I want to be," she said, grinning.

"Here comes Cody fresh from his warm-up." All of the association's horses have a work-out with a volunteer in the saddle well before the special riders begin. At the moment, Mandy's sorrel was out having a run and a chance to stretch his muscles. It would settle him down before they began their sedate walk around the corral.

Nabil, a local college student from Kuwait, was one of the volunteers. He led Dianne's mount around the high platform. Cody wore a piece of equipment called a *surcingle*, a special kind of girth circling his shoulders that made it easier for the rider to grab while getting on. Brian helped Dianne slide her right leg over Cody's back. She settled onto the padded blanket that replaced the saddle's seat and grasped the open-handled pommel with both hands. She was riding almost bareback, using only the front part of the surcingle and its stirrups, that was made especially for the handicapped. But During her thirty-minute ride, Dianne had to keep her feet free of the stirrups and exercise her dangling legs by swinging them to and fro. Next she'd give her arms a workout. Such movements build strength and endurance and are required of every rider in the program.

"Now I'm free to be me!" Dianne said. "And today I'm going to fly! Just watch me smile!"

She, Nabil, with George and Nancy, her side-walkers, headed for the ring. They circled the fence line for about ten minutes. She gained her sense of balance and self-control and soon completed her exercises. Because of having a strong upper torso as well as rugged determination, Dianne was then allowed to ride alone while the helpers watched. Her feet were now firmly in the stirrups. With great joy, everyone stopped to watch the former horsewoman boldly urge Cody into a slow canter. Deep inside they shared her feelings of accomplishment and pride. Dianne had what the old-timers called grit.

Seated atop one of the picnic tables with Alex, Skylyn had stopped sketching. Brushing the tears from their cheeks, they joined in the applause as a bright smile covered Dianne's face.

"See! I told you!" The fifty-one-year-old grandmother called out to all.

It was a good morning at Hopewell Farms.

Near noontime Brian helped them dismount directly behind their station wagon. Max stood stock-still, and showing the strain of a hot and tiring session, Mandy let herself be lifted off and carried to the front seat. He left the door open to catch the cool breeze.

After Dianne was down she asked for her cane. Using it with her left hand, she held on to the car with the other and inched her way toward the open driver's side door.

"I'm in this game to the end," she said. With Pam's guidance, she reached for the steering wheel, turned, and plopped into the seat in time to see their horses being led away. Max pulled at his lead trying to turn around.

"He doesn't want to go," George said to Pam.

"Wait a minute!" Mandy said. "Can you bring them back?" Both horses were happy to return. Max stuck his head in the door by Mandy and sniffed. Cody walked up to Dianne and nuzzled her arm.

"Searching for something, big guy?" she asked.

"They know we forgot their rewards," Mandy said, reaching

for Max's apple. Pam and George backed Max up and removed his bridle so he could chew his treat.

"He also has a halter on because he loves to stop and crop grass, and it becomes difficult for the riders to control him," Pam said. Max stuck his face into the car, and Mandy held out the welcome apple.

Wanting the pleasure of Cody's company to last a bit longer, Dianne had brought the biggest carrot she could find. She was determined to allow him only one bite at a time.

"It'll take him a while to finish it," she declared.

"Looks like a horse banquet to me," Pam said.

"And it's low fat," Dianne shot back.

With a hard chomp! Cody clamped his teeth on the carrot and pulled; Dianne held on, forcing him to bite off a hunk. He rolled it around in his mouth and began to munch on his snack. He worked on three more big chunks, finally demolishing the whole thing. The crowd cheered when both horses curled their lips and snuffled the dashboard, hoping for more.

"We're bonding," Mandy said, loving another chance to hug Max's neck.

Alex looked up and saw her mother and Aggie making their way toward them.

"Hi, Mom, you're early."

"We're finished for the day," Aggie said, greeting Pam, who introduced them around.

"Ready to go, honey?"

On the ride home Alex told her mother about the morning's events. Anne made a quick stop at McDonald's to order a couple of Big Macs with drinks and fries. Puzzled, Alex glanced at her.

"I thought you and Mrs.Eaglefeather were going to have lunch?" she asked. Anne held up her hand.

"Wait until we get our food and are clear of traffic. Then I'll explain. By the way," Anne said, "Aggie suggested getting a quilt show together for Hopewell Farms some Saturday. She'll ask Pam about it. She wants to include our heirloom quilts."

"Neat! Everyone will like that. Families can come and watch their riders and enjoy the show. And I know a certain someone who has plenty of them tucked away in a cedar chest at home!"

"Me, too!" Anne laughed. "How about unwrapping my burger," she said a few minutes later, taking a sip of her cola.

"Okay, sweetheart, I have something to tell you..." Sighing, she balanced her sandwich on the center arm rest.

"What?" Alex's head snapped up. "Something's wrong! I knew it! Mom, what is it?"

"Dad called me; it seems your grandfather is having stomach pains again and..."

"No," Alex whispered. "Poor Gramp." She turned toward her mother, needing eye contact. "Will he be all right?"

"Your father's called Dr. Cash—he's due within the hour, and I want to get there in time to talk to him."

"How bad are the pains?"

"He's not able to get comfortable lying down, sitting, or standing; nothing helps."

"He's really hurting then, because he never complains," Alex said. "Where are the boys?"

"Rob's mother took them to her house earlier this morning. We didn't want to upset them."

With her hand over her eyes, Alex leaned back against the seat. Mind swirling a mile a minute, she groped for her lunch and stuffed it all into the paper bag. She forced herself to voice her biggest concern: "Is it his heart?"

"We don't know." Anne took her hand. "Let's just say our prayers, and Alex dear, remember when we said we'd always try to think positively?" Anne saw the shimmer in her daughter's eyes when she whispered, "I remember. Just hurry, Mom."

On that beautiful sunny afternoon, Alexandra sat silent, hands folded, eyes closed during most of the trip. Thirty miles seemed like three hundred until they saw the beginning of Tanner land. Ten minutes later they turned into the lane, zipped through the open gate, and rounded the curve.

"Oh, I was afraid of that!" Anne said. There in the field next to the corral was a bright-red medivac helicopter, its rotors slowly whirring to a stop.

Alex jumped out and raced up the steps with her mother not far behind. She burst through the door and found three emergency technicians in blue coveralls working at a mobile gurney that held her very pale grandfather.

"Gramp!" she cried, shooting around a young woman struggling to untangle the long tubes connected to an intravenous bag of clear liquid dangling from a holder. She seized his hand. "We're here," she said, her voice wobbling. She leaned over to kiss his cheek. Are you still hurting?" Her gaze searched his face, begging him to speak.

He opened heavy-lidded eyes and gave her a wan smile. "I'm okay," he mumbled.

"He's had a shot to ease the pain," Steven said. His arm circled her shoulders just as Anne arrived, and he drew them aside. The medic was checking Gramp's hand to find a good vein for the IV needle.

"He got so bad after I talked to your mom, I had to call for help," Steven said, running his hand through his hair. "Emergency services made the decision to send in the helicopter. Doc will meet us in the emergency room."

"You're going with him, Dad?" Alex asked.

"There's no room for anyone else," he said, shaking his head. "I'll have to drive."

"Let me call Rob's mother to check on the twins," Anne said. "I'll put food out for Chester and Goldie and go with you."
She hustled toward the kitchen.

"Me, too!" Alex said. Steven paused, then nodded. "All right. I know better than to try talking you out of it."

"Mr. Tanner," an EMT said, "we're ready."

Steven nodded, spoke a few words to his dad, and went to hold the door for the gurney to roll through. One technician stead-

ied the swinging IV bag; another checked the pulse monitor taped to Gramp's left ring finger. Alexandra looked on, unable to move a muscle. She clamped her hand over her mouth. This couldn't be happening! The door swung closed. There was nothing but silence.

Something touched her ankle. She glanced down and found Chester, his tail tucked between his legs. She knelt beside him. "Gramp's sick, Chettie, and he's going to the hospital. You and Goldie have to stay here, little guy." Realizing what she had said, Alex jumped up, wrenched open the door and dashed out. Flying down the steps, she ran for all she was worth to catch up with the medical team moving toward the waiting helicopter.
Out of breath, she got there just as they bumped over the uneven grass around the corral.

"Wait!" she caught hold of the chrome rail, begging anyone who would listen. "I want to say good-bye!" Moving closer to the lazily churning blades, they nodded her on. "Keep your head down!" someone called. When they came to the open hatch, Gramp held out his hand.

"Hey, missie, I'll see you later. When I get better we'll hire this thing and take a ride."

"I'll hold you to it! See you in the hospital, I love you." She kissed him and backed away right into her dad's waiting arms. Two by two, the gurney's legs folded under as they pushed it into the helo; the EMTs followed. The door slid shut and the latch slammed into place, locking the passengers in. Alex let the tears flow. As soon as Steven guided them a safe distance away, the pilot signed thumbs up, revved the engine, and pushed the throttle forward.

Peeking over the fence, two curious colts under the care of Pete, a temporary stablehand, watched the goings-on. Both frisky yearlings raced to the far side of the paddock when the copter blades bit into the air, swirling dirt everywhere. With heavy hearts, the Tanners watched the huge craft lift off and move away with its precious cargo.

Alexandra stared after it, tracing its course in the sky until it disappeared over the mountains.

"Honey, let's go," her mother gently prompted. "We've got a long drive ahead of us."

"Emergency one: code blue! EM one:code blue!" The loudspeaker blared. Steven's head snapped up just as their feet hit the wide rubber mat, triggering a hidden switch. Whoosh! The huge double doors flew open. He strode down the hallway, through the crowded waiting room, and up to the reception desk. Following behind, Alex slipped a trembling hand into Anne's and clasped it tight.

"May I help you, sir?" a woman in white asked.

"Please," he said. "My father, Robert Tanner, was brought in about an hour ago. Dr. Cash was to meet him here. I'd like to know if there's any word on his condition."

"Certainly. If you'll have a seat in the waiting room," she said. "I'll try to find out something for you." Ten minutes later another nurse approached.

"Sir, they're still running tests on Mr. Tanner. It'll be a while until we know the results. Your doctor should be out shortly to speak to you."

"When will I be able to see my dad?"

"He's upstairs in X-ray right now. You can see him when they're finished."

"Tell him we're here, will you?" Steven said.

Alexandra and Anne watched TV in a quiet corner of the waiting room, trying hard to concentrate on a game show. After pacing the hall for what seemed like hours, Steve went outside, where his feet continued to pound the sidewalk. He made a decision and returned to his family.

"This hurry-up-and-wait situation irritates me, and I don't like it one bit," he said, standing with his hands on his hips. "I'm going after some answers; wait here, Alex!"

She watched him stalk off with her mother by his side. Exhausted, Alex took a deep breath and swiped her hand down her face to stifle a yawn. Oh, I can't stand it! It's like a horrible nightmare. What can I do? I need to think positively. She relaxed, allowing her mind to wander over some of the wonderful things she and Gramp had done over the years: the rodeo competition; their picnic ride; the beaver pond one glorious Christmas day. A prayer on her lips, she rested her head on her arms, and drifted off...

"Boy, missie, you and Jessie sure fly like the eagles. I think it's time for you to enter the rodeo."

"Maybe so, Gramp." She smiled at him, stretching her legs beside the red-and-white striped picnic cloth.

"Seventeen seconds flat! You did it! You're the winner!

"You helped, Gramp! You're a winner, too."

"It's icy cold; the baby beavers must be freezing in that lodge. Look at the cougar tracks, Gramp. Are they safe from hungry animals?"

It's cold, but they'll be okay. Their parents always take good care of them..."

"Alex!" Someone was bothering her, but she shrugged it off. "No, let me alone! I'm happy right where I am."

"Wake up! You'll be even happier—there's good news. Gramp's going to be okay. C'mon, wake up sleepyhead. You're right under the air conditioner, and your arms are like ice." Steven picked up Anne's sweater and draped it around her shoulders. She lifted her head and stared into her dad's eyes.

"What's happening?" she struggled to sit up. "How is he?"

"Comfortable now. He's had a bad gall bladder attack, and a gall stone lodged in front of the bile duct. That's what was giving him so much pain. It finally moved."

"Thank goodness." Alex sighed. "But, wait! Is the doctor sure it's not his heart?"

"They've done a ton of tests. Doc Cash says his heart's strong, but gall bladder problems sometime act like heart trouble and can be just as painful."

"He's had so much of it lately, and it happens right after he eats. What can they do to help that?"

"Good question, honey." He patted her arm. "Hey! You'd be a great doctor," he said. "They want him to rest for now; then if no more stones show up, they'll remove the gall bladder."

"Oh, now he has to go through that," she said, slapping the arm of her chair. "Give the poor man a break!"

"Calm down; no one said life's easy." He claimed the empty seat next to her. "After they remove it he won't be bothered with stones. Besides they now have a much simpler procedure using a laser: it's called *laparoscopy*."

"A lap-whatski?" She had to laugh.

"It's a new type of operation. Mom and I saw a video on it." Steven handed her a folder the doctor had given him. He pointed to the diagrams while explaining it. "A miniature camera and a pen-like laser probe are inserted in a few tiny incisions in the upper stomach area. The stones are suctioned out of the bladder, flattening it like an empty balloon. Then they slice it loose with the laser beam and pull it out through a small incision in the navel. That's it, boom! Over and done in an hour. And if everything goes right, he comes home the next day."

"Wow! Through his belly button? All right! Go for it! Can they do it tomorrow?"

"Let's hope so! You want to visit him?"

"How are you feeling?" Alex asked, giving him a hug.

"Pretty good, sweetie," he pushed the button to move the head of the bed a bit higher. Taking a sip of water, he held up the glass. "I'm celebrating—the pain's gone." He eased back on his pillow after Alex plumped it up for him. "But..." a frown wrinkled his forehead "I seem to have another problem." They leaned closer, waiting. "I think I lost my hat!" Their collective sigh could surely be heard all the way down the hall.

"You left it at home, silly." Alex laughed, swiping tears from her cheeks. "Anyway, I'm sure you won't need it when we take the helicopter ride you promised."

"Gee whiz, did I say that? Must have been the shot, or else I'm crazy. Let's stick with trucks or horses, honey. I don't ever want to ride in one of those overgrown eggbeaters again." He looked at his son. "No wonder I joined the army—jeeps make so much more sense!"

"I'm sure glad that's over." Steven sighed, pulling the Explorer to a stop in front of the house early Tuesday evening. "It's been a rough two days for everyone."

"I hope Gramp can get some rest tonight," Alex said, helping to unload the groceries.

"It's really just Band-Aid surgery. There are no stitches, and the three tiny incisions are merely covered with adhesive. So he'll soon be fit to travel," her mother added.

The twins rushed down the steps to meet them. "How's Gramp?"

"Well look who's here," Anne said, leaning down to greet them. "He's doing fine. He should be home tomorrow afternoon."

"Mrs. Stanley brought us back early, and she has dinner ready for you—it's baked chicken. We ate already."

"That sounds wonderful."

"Boys," Steven said, "Gramp wanted me to tell you that he remembers his promise to help you plant your flower garden."

"Good!" Chandler said. "Our seedlings are getting too tall."

"I don't think he should use the shovel right after his operation," Ty said. "Maybe he should just watch us."

"You're right," Steven added, handing him a jug of milk and Chandler a carton of orange juice to tote inside. "How about just letting him supervise the job, and we'll do the digging?"

"What time will you be home?" Steven asked Anne at breakfast.

"Alex has an early interview with a volunteer, and I need to talk with Pam about space for next Saturday's quilt show. We'll leave early and be back here for lunch, then we can rescue Gramp from his hospital bed."

"Let's take the twins with us and give Rita Stanley a break," Steven said.

Hopewell Farms was brimming with people. Alex chose a seat at one of the two picnic tables set aside for the adult students to eat their brown-bag lunches before riding.

"Good morning, Mr. Hall," Alex said when the tall gentleman ducked his head under a branch and came to sit on the bench across from her. "Thanks for taking time for me today."

"Glad to do it. Call me George like everyone else," he said with a twinkle in his eye.

"I have a two-part question. When did you first learn about Horses for the Handicapped, and how long have you been volunteering here?"

"I had a stroke over three years ago, and my doctor prescribed aquatic therapy at the YMCA," George said. "In the beginning I thought that I might never walk again, and I didn't care about anything. My wife talked me into meeting the swim instructor. I liked him so much I decided to try it. The months of warm water exercises with a therapist helped to strengthen my whole body.

"I soon had good enough results with my arms that they thought I might try something different, like this program. They told me that when you squeeze your legs against the horse's sides it strengthens the muscles."

He and Alex chatted about her favorite sport for another ten minutes. She discovered that his first visit was the only time he had ever been around horses.

"So, George," she said, " I guess it was then that you fell in love with riding."

"No sir! I rode just once and decided I didn't like it at all!"

"What happened?"

"Simple story. I guess I should have given it more time, but I never felt in charge. I thought the horse had control," he admitted.

Alex went with him to help Raven and Pam lift Jill onto her mount.

"Just five weeks to go then those casts are history, little gal!" he said.

"I can't wait," Jill said. "Then I go to water therapy just the way you did. After that I'll come back here to learn how to ride all over again. In a few more months I'll be back on my own horse."

George answered the second part of Alex's question as he adjusted the youngster's straps. He had continued with the pool therapy for many months. He and his wife began daily walking program that soon turned into a two-mile trek.

"Thank heaven it all resulted in a complete recovery," he said, inviting Alex to come along to the corral. "I discovered how it felt to be disabled and have wonderful people help me overcome it. Now I'm returning the favor by helping others."
He unhooked the gate for Raven to take her horse through, relatched it, and paused with his foot on the bottom rail.

"Besides, I get my exercise three times a week right here going around in the best of circles!" He joined them when Raven jogged by, guiding Apple Pie on their first pass, with Jill content for the moment to follow the well-worn path along the fence.

"Welcome Home, Gramp!" read the colorful sign suspended between two of the front-porch pillars. Red and green balloons surrounded the banner.

"Well, look at that! And balloons, too! Who did all the work?"

"We did," the twins chimed in. "We just blew and blew, and Dad helped. But Alex said she used her computer to blow up your sign!" Their words tumbled out as they unbuckled their seatbelts. "Someday she promised to teach us how to do that. She let us color it! Do you like it, Gramp?"

"I love it! You sure know how to make your ole grandpa feel special. Thanks, guys. Is that a picture of a helicopter I see next to the banner?"

"Yes," Chandler said. "Ty and I drew it! Dad told us one landed right here, and you flew to the hospital in it."

"And, and...Gramp?" Tyler asked, throwing his arms around his grampa's neck. "Would you tell us all about it?"

"Harump." He cleared his throat. "I'm really trying to forget it, Ty, but I guess I could do it for my three best pals." He winked at Alexandra and reached for her hand. "Thanks for my sign, honey. You're wonderful, and you did a great job." Alex merely looked at him and squeezed back, hard.

Hopewell News

The Eaglefeathers pulled into Hopewell Farms bright and early Saturday morning.

"There's Gramp Tanner; he must be feeling better," Skylyn said. They watched him take a coil of rope and his carpenter's pouch from the Jeep. He waved to them as he started for the barn.

"He's hard at work as usual. I'm glad he got over the surgery without a problem," Aggie said, waving back. She reminded Sky not to disappear. She needed help unloading the boxes.

Joe found Steven and Anne fixing a space to hang some of Gramp's prized quilts. They were in a section of the barn that the young volunteers had scrubbed clean.

"It's starting to look great," Joseph said, poking his head through the doorway.

"Good, the help has arrived," Steven said from up on the ladder. "How about handing me that can of nails." Joe snagged the container and held it up to his friend.

"Your spot's in the breezeway, Joe," Anne said from her own

perch on a ladder. "I think Aggie'll like it. You can walk around both sides of her work, and it's also protected."

"Anne came up with the idea of using wooden clothes rods as hangers," Steve said, motioning for Joseph to send one up to him. "I think it'll work pretty well. We've got plenty of extras if you need any."

"Thanks, but I've dusted off some of Aggie's old display racks from the early days of local art shows."

Steven pounded an eight-penny nail halfway into the planking.

"Okay, let's see what happens." He laid one end of the pole over the nail. Anne settled the other on her side and climbed down.

"I had to iron every single quilt because they've been folded up in Gramp's wooden chests for years. Then I got some of these from the carpet store." She held out a six-foot cardboard roller to Joe. He helped her shake out a cream beauty with a traditional pinwheel design done in multicolors.

"The show's advertised in this morning's paper. Maybe Pam'll get some more volunteers if a lot of people come."

"That's the whole idea. Many don't even know the organization exists. I'll show you Aggie's spot just as soon as we get this hung." Anne handed a corner of the quilt to Steven, and Joseph climbed up to slide the other end over the rod.

"Super!" she said, handing them a few small squares of muslin and some clips. "Put them on each side over the cotton patches to hold it in place."

"This is perfect for children's quilts, Sky," Alexandra said, tapping her pencil on her pad as she wandered through the clothesline display. "Our white-on-white baby quilt with the French-knot embroidery is my favorite. I love those puffy flowers. Mom says that way of sewing them is called *trapunto*. There's cotton batting stuffed inside them," she said. "Someday I'll learn to do it. I get such a good feeling thinking about the love my great-grandmother put into every tiny stitch."

"NanEagle says we hold cherished family memories in our

hearts," Sky said. "I feel that way about her stories; they're so precious to me, along with her baskets and my mother's weavings."

"I'm glad the crib quilts are here in the tack room," Alex said. "Especially since it's our favorite place on the whole farm," Sky added. She put her head down and got back to sketching, savoring the fun they'd had cleaning it up, making it come alive.

"Our little quilts have a long history: Gramp says they've been handed down through generations of Tanners. This one was his Christening quilt and later his brother's. Then he and Grandma used it for my father's ceremony. Not to be outdone, Mother said she wrapped me in it for my baptism, too." Alex grinned, and twirled around on her booted toes

"That's awesome, Al." Sky paused at her task. "You can't buy that kind of history, but you're living it."

"What a nice thought! Alex sat down on the bench beside her friend. "You'll enjoy this one, too— I remember the twins' baptism when Mom draped it over them. I stood between my parents and shared that special time. Dad was holding Chandler. He squirmed and howled through it all. Mom had Tyler, but he slept during the whole thing. Dad teases Chan that the font must have held ice water because he still fights his bath!"

"They were true to form then!" Sky said with a chuckle.

"Your sketch is coming along nicely. Our families will love it. Set a drawing aside for my next column, will you?" Sky nodded.

"I think I'll give it a water-color wash when I get home," Sky said. "The blue comforter next to your little white one will look perfect against the old wood background."

Visitors to the show could also watch horses and riders doing their exercises in both corrals. The rider atop Flip, a flaxen-coated palomino, squirmed in the saddle and fidgeted with his safety hat. Pam stopped the horse, taking time to encourage him before she tossed six brilliantly colored rubber disks high in the air. Flying like frisbees they landed in different spots, decorating the churned brown earth.

"Blue!" Pam called out. "Blue, Chris!" she reinforced the command. "I want you to point Flip toward the blue circle. Come on now, concentrate!" Chris slowly drew his attention back to what was usually his favorite game. He pulled the reins to the left, and Flip dutifully turned toward the appropriate disk.

"Good for you!" Pam congratulated him at each success, quickly scooping up the prize and handing it to him. "Two more to go!"

Moving Flip toward a circle, Chris hand-signed his thoughts to Pam. "I know," she reassured him. "Just one more, and you can go see the show you've been angling to visit. Now find the yellow one!"

Onlookers clapped as he achieved his goal. Grinning, he held all six trophies on his lap and rode out of the corral. He signed to his caretaker, Rebecca, and she waved back at her favorite young man.

Always there for her people and always on the run, Pam hurried to the next ring to oversee the not-so-fast-paced game in progress. She unlatched the gate in time to witness the riders throw their dice. They cast large black-foam cubes that bobbled and bounced to a stop in front of their mounts. Margaret's toss turned up four white dots. She urged her horse four paces ahead. Throughout the game, all five riders pitched the dice, with their leaders calling the numbers, reminding them to count the matching number of their horses' footfalls. Step by step, they moved along, each chanting numbers.

"A single step is the hardest for your horse to take!" Pam reminded them. "You need to use firm control!"

"We know!" they groaned.

"Good, Margaret!" she said to the older woman, who had ridden horses since she was a child. "You're in the lead! Come on, people, toss again! You need to catch up!" Progressing at a snail's pace after each roll, they took their mounts to the opposite end of the corral and turned back.

"Margaret wins!" Pam declared. "And guess what! Today's her birthday, so it's an extra happy one for her." Pleased at being chosen to lead the parade out of the ring, Margaret beamed when they serenaded her and waved her thanks. Her saddle creaked as she leaned over, confessing to Pam that she was sixty-four! Pam promised to keep her secret.

High noon came quickly to Hopewell Farms that day.

"Alex! Sky!" Pam called, beckoning them to the picnic tables. "Come and see what we have!"

The girls made their way to the area both had used all month and jokingly dubbed their "office."

"Here you go, nice job!" Pam said, handing them copies of their newsletter. Alex found her photo on the front page along with those of their co-workers. The headline declared: *New Youth Volunteers Do Make a Difference*!

"Super!" Sky said. "Where's your column, Al?"

"I almost forgot," she said and flipped through to discover the article bearing her very own byline.

"'Tack Talk,' by Alexandra Tanner," she read aloud. Clutching the paper close to her chest, she looked at her friend.
"Wow," was all she could say.

"'Hopewell's Face painting Fridays are a huge success.'" Sky read Alex's opening line. "Great start, Al!" she said, continuing on to find another surprise. "Look! Here's my clown drawing of Mr. Yeager and another of Jill." She found a perfect likeness of Chris and another of Margaret, both working hard.

"Here's a real beaut of Dianne feeding Cody his carrot!" Alex pointed out. "Sky! They've used your art throughout the whole issue!" It was Sky's turn to say, "Wow!"

Sometimes Horses for the Handicapped received money to help fund its work—blankets, saddles, and other equipment came as welcome donations. They were blessed from time to time with the gift of a horse. The staff considered itself fortunate whenever veterinarians had time to volunteer their services. But Pam was especially generous in complementing the girls' help and wonderfully artistic ideas that made their job so much more fun. She was proud of riders and workers alike.

"You're a big part of our volunteer family," she said to Sky and Alex. "We thank you for being leaders in your own quiet way, even if you aren't old enough to lead the riders yet. And believe me, I know what kind of horsewomen you are! I can't wait to see what you accomplish when you're sixteen!"

Overcome, Skylyn and Alexandra could only murmur a polite thank you. They were quite unaware that a crowd of assistants with their riders and horses had gathered, encircling them and their delighted families.

It was indeed a very good day at Hopewell Farms.

The end.

Friends Forever

Marilyn Martin